The Mediterranean Mystery

By

Malcolm C Brooks

The Mediterranean Mystery

Author: Malcolm C Brooks

Copyright © Malcolm C Brooks (2023)

The right of Malcolm C Brooks to be identified as author of this work has been asserted by the author in accordance with section 77 and 78 of the Copyright, Designs and Patents Act 1988.

First Published in 2023

ISBN 978-1-915796-35-6 (Paperback)

Book layout by:
> White Magic Studios
> www.whitemagicstudios.co.uk

Cover Design by: Chris Saunders

Published by:
> Maple Publishers
> Fairbourne Drive
> Atterbury
> Milton Keynes
> MK10 9RG
> www.maplepublishers.com

Malcolm C Brooks

RAF CYPRUS 1958

Malcolm is 84 years old and lives a very busy life. He now coaches pétanque at Cricklade Pétanque Club.

Last year he was awarded 'Great Western Regional Coach of the Year'

This book is mainly set in Cyprus, a country dear to his heart even though he was almost murdered or killed there on numerous occasions.

Malcolm spent 1957-1960 in Cyprus with the RAF.

He recently wrote a memoir cataloguing his life-threatening narrow escapes and below are examples of a few:

- On bringing a lorry load of ammunition from Farmagusta Docks to the RAF base, a bomb exploded literally just yards in front of his vehicle. It left a smoking crater immediately in front of his lorry but he managed to return it to base.

- Then there was the time a group of EOKA terrorists hurled bombs at him -

- Just a few months later on Remembrance Day the EOKA blew up his NAAFI - three servicemen were killed during this attack and twenty others badly injured. (Fortuitously, Malcolm had spent extra time cleaning his boots before going over that evening, ready for the following day's inspection - so escaped injury!)

- Not in uniform, he was detailed to pick up an RAF pilot who lived in the Greek half. En route a British Military policeman was set on shooting him mistaking him for a Greek terrorist. Only when he yelled out, "I'm Bloody English," in his unmistakeable accent, the gun was eventually dropped from the small of his back and he was allowed to go on ...

- He was given a leave pass home for his 21st birthday but while flying over France noticed billowing smoke then huge flames flaring from one of the plane's engines. The Beverley made an emergency crash landing on a small airstrip over France. Three of his leave days were swallowed up waiting for a replacement plane - but he was alive.

He considers himself lucky to have survived and lives life to the full.

To Celia

"El chariclo"

M C Brooke

Main Character List

Two detectives: Harry Webb and Andrew Brown

The DCS: John Street

Secretary: Angela

Murdered man and his ex wife: Mr and Mrs Dimitris Pantazis

Lady on beach: Winnie Williams

Deckchair attendant: Tom Wilson

Waiter: Eugene

Winnie's neighbour: Mary Mills

Winnie's sister and brother in law: Linda and Clive Bowman

Two garage mechanics: Alex and Stan

Garage owner and his wife: Max and Jane Grey

Police Chief in Cyprus: Chief Yiannis Galanis

Two murder suspects: Yirgos Papadopoulos and Andreas Athanasiou

Dimitris Pantazis' ex business partner: Mr Nico Castellanos

Restaurant owner in Cyprus: Zaikai

Dimitris Pantazis' partner: Mrs Angie Sakalis

Mrs Sakalis's Daughter: Chloe

(Places are real but all characters are fictitious, any resemblances are purely coincidental - but in such an instance the author would love to meet them!)

Contents

Chapter 1

Unserendipiosity

*S*ometimes, *don't you think, things, scenes are just a tad too perfect to be true or lasting? I am sure Lewis Carroll could have created the perfect word for such a phenomenon ... 'Unserendipiosity' or the like.*

The last piece of the jigsaw puzzle you see just did not fit. It was the wrong shape, the wrong colour. The scene was that of an idyllic English seaside resort with everything dovetailing beautifully: gorgeous weather; happy scantily dressed holiday makers; gentle blue waves lapping the shore making the young children giggle and jump as the cool water cheekily threatened their toes but then ... the incongruously dressed gentleman appeared on the scene. What was he doing there? He simply did not fit in ...

It was a really sunny day in Brighton. The sky was a gorgeous hazy blue featuring one or two cumulus clouds. The sea was calm and bathers were splashing randomly while the more adventurous visitors raced their paddle boards.

The beach was now beginning to fill and Tom Wilson the deckchair attendant was happy as the more people who wanted to hire from him the more his takings grew. Tom worked the beach during the summer holidays. He really enjoyed his job as he loved meeting people as well as having the freedom of working in shorts and tee shirt most days. Perfect. Just perfect!

The cycle path was heaving with youngsters on electric scooters and skateboards, while on the promenade crowds were talking, walking or simply sat enjoying the sea air. A beautiful snapshot of life in a typical English resort - apart from on one of the deckchairs by the promenade, just opposite The Grand hotel, was an incongruously dressed gentleman. He was indeed very smart wearing a dark blue well pressed shirt and trousers, a dark grey jacket, brown brogues, a straw hat and sunglasses. He was also sporting a Mediterranean tan. But somehow, today, well, he looked as though he should have been somewhere else, not there.

Around mid morning Winnie walked purposefully along the beach. She did so at least three or four times a week, on each occasion carrying a large bag and politely approaching holidaymakers asking for their loose change 'to buy a coffee'.

She commenced her walk from the beach huts at Hove to the Palace Pier and some days would venture as far as the Brighton Marina. On a good day the pickings were rich. The police were well aware of her habitual trait but turned a blind eye as she had a pleasant demeanour and never ever hassled anyone.

Winnie was very friendly with Tom and often stopped to have a chat with him so today she asked about the smartly dressed gentleman in the deckchair by the promenade. Tom told her he had paid for an all day ticket.

After saying her farewells to Tom, Winnie approached the gentleman in the deckchair with a smile and politely asked if he had any loose change for a coffee.

"Hello. Yes, of course," he smiled back. He stood up, emptied both trouser pockets giving her two huge handfuls of £1 and £2 coins and a few euros.

Winnie thanked him kindly but questioned whether it was too much.

"No," he replied, "I don't need it so please take it all," he smiled.

Winnie thanked him again and continued along to the Palace Pier asking others along the way for coffee money. Many donated to her cause.

When she arrived at the pier she did exactly as she always did - made for the public toilets and changed from her scruffy old clothes into a very smart floral 'A line' dress accessorised with light red kitten heeled summer shoes carefully taken from her bag. She then crossed the road to her favourite restaurant in the Old Ship hotel.

As she approached the Mess Deck, Eugene, one of the waiters who knew her by sight, welcomed her and offered her a seat by the window. He asked if she would like her usual bar menu.

"No, not today thank you Eugene. I will choose from the 'a la carte' menu please. I would like a starter of Halloumi then Scampi, chips and salad for the main course. Oh, and a large, cool glass of Sauvignon Blanc."

"Of course Winnie. We have a delightful Marlborough Sauvignon in our cellar," advised Eugene, wearing his sommelier hat.

Winnie had enjoyed an exceptional day. So many had been generous along the beach, not just the suited gentleman so she indulged herself to the rarest of treats. Silently she toasted her success, thanked Eugene and left.

... And so it was time for her to cross the road, revisit the public toilets, change back into her scruffy dress, old jacket and down at heel sandals before recommencing yet another, hopefully lucrative walk back along the beach.

When she reached the deckchair area she told Tom of her very special lunch served with a glass of the best Marlborough Sauvignon.

"It sounds lovely," Tom enthused, "one day I will have to join you."

"Yes," agreed Winnie. "That would be great. I look forward to it very much! Oh, by the way, did the gentleman in the deckchair get up at all? Is he alright?"

"No, he hasn't moved. He must be having a good sleep under that beach towel!"

"Strange," mused Winnie. "I must have a word with him and thank him for contributing to my meal today."

She gingerly approached the gentleman tapping him lightly on the shoulder. As she did so his head slumped forward and the beach towel fell to the ground, revealing horrific blood-saturated clothing over his chest.

Winnie screamed hysterically ... over and over and over ... more piercing with every breath - dropping her bag and holding her head tightly between her two hands as she did so but this failed to contain her terrified shrieks.

Tom came running up to console her. He quickly pulled the beach towel back over the man's chest and head.

Two athletic joggers passing by heard her blood curdling screams. Fortunately they were paramedics from the Royal Sussex hospital and stopped to help. One placed a finger on the man's neck to feel for a pulse but there wasn't one. He had been murdered. The paramedic careful covered the man's face again as the crowds gathered.

Meanwhile the other paramedic dialled 999 for police and ambulance. Almost immediately two police cars sped along the promenade followed by an ambulance - all vehicles with their blue lights flashing and sirens blazing.

How an idyllic seaside scene can change in a matter of minutes!

The first uniformed officers ran to where Winnie, Tom Wilson and the two paramedics were frantically waving for their attention. The paramedics explained they had been on their jog when they heard the bloodcurdling screams. They had gone over to offer assistance and there they were confronted with the heavily bloodstained victim.

"We checked his pulse but instinctively knew he was dead. It looked as though he had been either stabbed or shot in the chest but we did not disturb the body. We covered his face with the beach towel to afford his privacy and dignity. We then tried to console the poor lady who found him as she was hysterical and in deep shock."

The uniformed police officer thanked the two paramedics and asked if they would leave their details with the other officer. They would of course then have to go to the station for fingerprinting at some point for the process of elimination.

The other two police officers quickly cordoned off the area with blue and white police tape and radioed the station for a tent to be sent down immediately.

The ambulance crew tried to persuade Winnie to come into their vehicle to treat her for shock but she insisted she was alright now and asked if she could just go home please. They agreed but explained the police would first need her to give a short statement.

After providing her personal details to the two officers Winnie Williams explained she had asked the unfortunate gentleman that morning for some money for a coffee. He had been extremely generous and given her enough for a meal so on the way back she went over to thank him once more. It was when she gently touched his shoulder for his attention the beach towel fell away and she saw all the blood. An awful lot of blood. It was horrible. Too horrible for words so she had screamed and screamed. All over his chest it was, the blood, all over ...

"That's fine Winnie, thank you. You can go home now. You will receive a visit from one of our officers in a day or two when they carry out their more thorough investigations. Would you like us to take you home?"

Winnie told them she was okay, thanked them anyway and after saying her goodbyes made her way slowly home.

Tom Wilson was back looking after the deckchairs when the police asked him if he was alright. He said he would be happier after he could call his dad to come down with him. Tom gave the police his full name, Thomas Charles Wilson. He confirmed he was still living with his dad and passed on his address and mobile number.

The two paramedic joggers were preparing to leave when one of the police officers realised he hadn't yet got their details.

"My name is Julian Robinson," said one, "and this is my husband John Hicks. We both live at the same address in Kemp Town." He gave their address and both mobile numbers.

The forensic officers had finished their job and were ready to pack up. They put a call through to the detective chief superintendent who asked that the ambulance take the body directly to the police morgue. He also instructed them to take the deckchair for further examination.

After they left the police tent was swiftly dismantled and loaded up for its return. The police tape however was left around the crime scene, which was cordoned off from the general public.

DCS John Street asked for all reports to be available first thing in the morning when he would consult his investigating team.

Chapter 2

'If you don't know where you are going any road will take you there'

Next morning DCS Street read the uniformed officers' reports along with the forensic reports and called in his secretary. "Angela," he announced, "this looks like a job for DCI Harry Webb ...

Would you please contact him and ask him to come to my office as soon as possible - if not sooner. Also locate young police officer Andrew Brown. You won't know him - he has only just joined us from the London Metropolitan police I would like him to work on this case alongside Harry. It will give him good experience and build his confidence. Then please call forensics. I'm very concerned about this case as we have absolutely no information on the victim's identity. Can you please check if his clothing was thoroughly searched for any identification marks or clues no matter how minute?"

"Yes Sir," I will call them as soon as I have located Harry Webb."

Angela eventually got through to Harry who was investigating a robbery at a house on the London Road. She informed him he was to immediately drop what he was doing for an urgent meeting with the DCS in regard of a murder. Harry swiftly passed the reins to his colleagues and was off.

Next Angela phoned forensics and asked the DCS's pertinent questions.

Seconds later she was in his office. "Sir, I have contacted Harry Webb who is on his way. I also located Andrew Brown who is sat waiting in the side office as we speak. When I spoke to forensics they confirmed there was no form of identification in any of the victim's clothes. His pockets were all empty. He had no birth marks on his body. So to sum up: no mobile; no wallet; no loose change and no birth marks. The victim was shot. Forensics will be sending you a report of the bullet used as and when."

"Thank you Angela. I will discuss all this with Harry."

Harry sailed into Angela's office just a couple of minutes later. He was tall, dark haired and slim in stature, neatly dressed with a pleasant disposition and a keen eye for detail. Truly proficient at this job. He was very much on the button and immediately wanted to know what was going on.

"I'm sorry Harry," Angela responded with a cheeky smile, "but you know very well I cannot discuss any confidential information. Tut! Tut! Very naughty!"

Harry laughed. He had a wicked sense of humour and loved to wind Angela up. He knocked and entered the superintendent's office. DCS John Street asked him to take a seat.

Angela gave them a few minutes before showing in police officer Andrew Brown. He was young, fresh faced with shortly cropped fair hair. He was keen and alert just a little shorter than Harry but muscular in stature, no doubt, Harry observed, an attribute achieved by regular workouts at the gym.

"Thank you both for coming to this urgent meeting," greeted the DCS. "Firstly Harry I want to introduce you to police officer Andrew Brown. Andrew's home town is Newcastle. He has been through the Metropolitan Training School, passed all his exams with distinction and qualified as a first class marksman on the shooting range. Andrew is keen to get involved in some active detective work. Do you have any problems with that Harry?"

"Not at all Sir. I would be pleased to have a younger, more athletic man working with me as I can't run as fast as I used too," Harry laughed.

"Thanks Harry, so let's get started. A situation like this is rare on our patch - the shooting on Brighton beach of an unidentified male probably of Mediterranean origin - (I mention this as I feel it will have a strong baring on this case) - and carrying absolutely no personal effects whatsoever.

Angela has emailed you both a copy of the police reports from SOCO along with a copy of the forensics report and a photograph of the deceased. I have received a further update from forensics a couple of minutes ago. They confirm the post-mortem shows the deceased man was shot cleanly through the heart with a .25 colt fitted with a silencer.

What have you heard about the incident via social media? Is anything being reported?"

"I have a news streaming app on my mobile Sir. It confirmed a man had been found dead in a deckchair on Brighton beach," volunteered Andrew, "and police have asked for any eyewitnesses to come forward. It concludes a statement will be issued later. That's all they gave out Sir."

"Well, they have that pretty accurate. You will see from the reports you have in your possession a woman, Winnie Williams, approached him, saw the blood and went completely hysterical and into deep shock. This prompted the deckchair attendant, Tom Wilson to run over to see what the commotion was about. Two male joggers also stopped to help. Fortunately they were paramedics from the Royal Sussex County Hospital so automatically took charge of the situation. They checked the victim's pulse, there wasn't one so pronounced him dead on the scene. They then called 999 for police and ambulance.

You have in your reports all the names, addresses and either home or mobile telephone numbers of those who were on the scene for you to follow up. So to recap - in the forensic report released this morning they confirm in fuller detail that no form of identification was found on the man: no mobile, no credit cards; no car keys; no notes or loose change.

This is ringing alarm bells with me - it could well be a very well executed and premeditated attack. But by who? Our dead man is probably of Greek or Turkish origin which would bring Cyprus well into the equation also.

He was wearing very expensive clothing and looked extremely fit and healthy. We presume he is a visitor here as no one has reported a missing person bearing his description and his clothing was not the kind a local would wear to the beach. On that assumption he may well have booked into one of the hotels or b&bs along the promenade. He may have a hire car parked up somewhere or he may have come here by train or National Express. So Harry where do you intend to start?"

"Well Sir, as that famous saying goes, 'If you don't know where you are going any road will take you there,' but I think

19

I will begin by looking at all CCTV footage commencing with that from the i360 tower. We should get a really good panoramic coverage for that area. If we do make a positive sighting, depending on which direction he is walking, we will check out every hotel in that vicinity."

"Who's attributed to that saying you just quoted then Harry?" Harry shrugged his shoulders.

"Can't recall at the moment."

"Well when you do remember let me know and as soon as you get any information on this case, no matter how small, text me immediately. I am deeply concerned about this - I have a strange feeling in my bones ... Do not take any chances as I can always send backup. The armoury have already been informed both you and police officer Brown may need to carry guns should the situation warrant it. I have authorised this.

Well good luck with this gentlemen. Remember it is imperative you keep me fully informed of your progress."

"Right Andrew your first big one, let's go," enthused Harry, "and always remember ' ... without fear of favour ...'" Andrew nodded, yes, he remembered his oath well.

As they left the station and made their way to the carpark Harry told Andrew he had a new silver BMW fitted out as an unmarked police car - with blues that could be employed. Eyes agog Andrew asked Harry if he could drive.

"Yes Andrew, you can."

"Thank you Sir." replied Andrew enthusiastically.

"Please don't refer to me as 'Sir' when we are out of the office Andrew. I am happy for you to call me Harry.

I think we should head for the i360 tower first. We could pull into one of the many parking areas nearby but I think before we go to view their CCTV we should firstly drive down to the beach to have a little chat with Tom Wilson. I would like to get an exact timing if possible on when he let the deckchair in question also ask him if he noticed anyone behaving strangely near the Mediterranean gentleman."

Andrew parked up and they walked along the beach to the deckchair area. It was absolutely heaving when they caught up with Tom Wilson.

Harry introduced himself and Andrew Brown, showing him their ID cards.

"All we want to know today Tom is what time did you give the unfortunate gentleman his hire ticket, also did you notice anyone else hanging around at midday yesterday, anyone at all?"

"That's no problem Sir. I'm pretty certain I issued his ticket at about 9.45am. When I asked him how long he wanted to hire it for he said he would need it for the day and would I accept euros. I told him I had no problem with euros and it would cost him £15. He gave me €20 and said to keep the change.

I didn't notice anyone hanging around but I wasn't there all the time as I always go to the Meeting Place cafe for a coffee and my lunch. I went there yesterday at about 12.30 and returned about 1.20."

"Did he take the €20 euro note from his pocket or from a wallet?"

"I couldn't say for sure but the note was pristine so I would guess from a wallet."

"Have you seen Winnie today?"

"No Sir."

"Thank you very much for your accurate timings Tom. We will follow that up now with the CCTV in the i360 tower."

As they approached the tower one of the staff, Jane Coleman, asked if they wanted to book a ride to the top.

"No, not today," replied Harry. "We are police detectives and would like to view your CCTV film from yesterday please."

"Yes Sir, but first I would have to see your identity cards."

Harry and Andrew both produced their cards for inspection.

"Thank you Sir, if you would like to follow me we will go down to the lower office and I will introduce you to Mr Tomkins. He is the man in charge ... Here we are." She knocked on the door and Harry and Andrew followed her in.

"Mr Tomkins, this is police detective Harry Webb and his assistant officer Andrew Brown. They would like to view the CCTV from yesterday."

"Of course Jane, no problem."

He walked over to the desk. "First of all do you have any specific time of day Sir?"

"Yes," Harry replied, "between 9am and 10am and again between 12.15 and 1.30."

"Okay. Right. I will rewind it to early morning yesterday." He deftly pushed a few buttons. "Here we go. This is from 9am. If you would both like to sit over here and just tell me when to stop the footage."

Both Harry and Andrew watched the screen intently. Andrew commented, "Wow! A very clear picture with an absolutely remarkable view."

It didn't take long before Harry shouted, "Stop! That's our man, just about to cross the road by the traffic lights." He looked towards Andrew for confirmation.

Andrew nodded in agreement. "Yes he is wearing the straw hat and sunglasses and is impeccably dressed."

"Can you print us any photographs from this film?" asked Harry.

"Yes Sir. Just make a note of the precise times and I will email them to you."

"Thank you. Could we have one of him at the traffic lights at 9.38am and could you just take the film back slightly to determine which direction he approached the lights please? Was it from the east or west?"

It didn't take long to spot him walking from the westerly direction just by Brunswick Terrace. Quite feasibly he could have either parked there or stayed in nearby accommodation.

Annoyingly they still had no clue as there were no hotel keys on him.

"Could you now run fast forward to about 9.45am? I would like to see him by the deckchair attendant?" He did so.

"Thank you ... Now! Now! Stop! Take it slower." Mr Tomkins obliged.

"... There he is Andrew! Just by the deckchairs talking to Tom Wilson. A shame he is taking the deckchair to the promenade wall as it's not easy to see over there."

Mr Tomkins fingers hovered in anticipation over the controls ...

"Now if we could just run forward from 12.30 and on to 1.30?" Mr Tomkins deftly did so, taking it slower though - anticipating Harry's impending orders.

"Andrew, look at this! Two men walking by wearing black tops and black baseball hats ... and one is carrying a beach towel! Yes! It's difficult to see their faces ... it's almost a rear view. We might get a front view from the CCTV from either The Grand or The Metropolitan hotels. Let's go!" He and Andrew jumped up from their seats.

"Thank you very much for your help Mr Tomkins, if you would please send on the photos - I have jotted down the times. My assistant here will give you his email address."

"Fine, no problem Sir. I take it that was the man who was murdered in the deckchair yesterday?"

"Sorry, I cannot comment on that. Suffice to say it is an ongoing investigation Mr Tomkins but thanks once again for your invaluable help today."

"Okay Sir I understand," replied Mr Tomkins proudly, "if I can help you with anything else please let me know. I am here most days." Harry nodded.

"Right Andrew onwards and upwards! I think we will go down as far as the beach huts. We can park up there and call in on Winnie Williams. I should think she will be at home as Tom said he hadn't seen her this morning. Then we will plough through the hotels and guest houses starting from the west with the Best Western all the way to The Grand if necessary."

Andrew dutifully parked the car near the beach huts and they walked across to where Winnie lived. She was at number 8 on the end of a block of sea view apartments.

As they approached Harry exclaimed, "Oh no. Hold it Andrew! Look! Her door is slightly ajar and it looks as though the lock has been forced too, see? The frame is splintered. Go back to the car and fetch the white linen gloves." Andrew was gone and back in a trice.

Harry silently pushed the door open and they both crept through.

"What a mess Harry, this place has been ransacked - clothes and papers everywhere. Someone has been searching for something in here, that's for sure!"

Harry looked in the bedroom. There was no sign of Winnie. Andrew went to check the phone and found the wires had been cut.

... Then, they heard the front door slowly creek open ... they gingerly inched their way to it, ready to pounce ... Harry gave the signal ...

... an old lady on crutches stood there! She lived in the apartment next door. They breathed again. She asked in a shaky voice if they were the police.

"Yes, we are police detectives my dear," Harry assured her kindly, "and have called to have a word with Winnie Williams."

The lady, who was wearing a long pink winceyette dressing gown with a rubber hot water bottle peeping out of one of its two enormous pockets, along with countless other things, explained Winnie had just been rushed off to hospital.

"Can you tell us what happened to her?" asked Harry gently.

"Yes, of course, if you will just help me back to my lounge then I will give you the details. I'm a bit unsteady on my feet you see. I fall a lot. Silly me! I do fall a lot."

Harry and Andrew carefully helped her back to her apartment and into her armchair, then formally introduced themselves.

The lady said she was Mary Mills and Winnie Williams had been her neighbour for the last three years. She was suffering from a nasty foot infection so Winnie had been kindly helping her out every morning with getting her dressed and applying fresh bandaging. Winnie had called in yesterday evening and told her the grim story of what had happened on the beach. When she left she promised to call in at 8.30 in the morning to change her bandages again.

Mary became very emotional when she explained to them both that it had gone past nine o'clock with no sign of Winnie and she was always so very punctual. She tried phoning her but her line was dead so she hobbled round, found Winnie's door open and Winnie just lying there all bloody and motionless on the floor.

She tried speaking to her as she was semiconscious. It looked as though she had been badly beaten up. She had black eyes and cuts and bruises all over her face and arms. Winnie told her two men had broken in the front door last night and demanded she tell them where the euros were. Winnie explained she did not have a clue what they were talking about but they didn't believe her and punched her repeatedly. Mary told her she would go back home and phone for an ambulance.

At that point Winnie lost consciousness. An ambulance had arrived very quickly and rushed her to the Royal Sussex County hospital.

Mary had phoned them to make sure she was alright but they would not give her any information at all about her friend, no matter which nurse she got through to and she had rung several!

She explained to Harry when she dialled 999 she thought she had asked for police and ambulance but she was all confused and shaken and may have just asked for an ambulance. It was all a bit of a blur. Things did get blurry sometimes, well often as a matter of fact. Some much more blurry than others, more like pea-souper fogs! Did he ever get that? Harry shook his head, smiling sympathetically and let her continue. They never did when she was younger either. Just like she never fell when she was younger. She could remember that. Most odd - all those years ago too and she could remember that!

"Okay Mary, police detective Andrew Brown and myself will sort this out and will make sure a nurse comes to bandage your foot soon. We will be in Winnie's apartment for some time and will certainly keep you informed."

Harry paused for a moment in deep reverie, pondering the information Mary had supplied. "Right Andrew, I want you to go straight back to the beach and find Tom Wilson. I am very concerned these two men may try to attack him next. Ask Tom if his dad would come down and spend the day with him. If he isn't able tell Tom to speak to his boss and ask for a few days off work. There's bound to be someone who can cover for him. Then tell him to go straight home and lock his doors.

Just give him a brief outline of what happened to Winnie but ask him not to tell another soul. It is important we keep this quiet. Stay with him until he gets sorted one way or the other."

"Okay Harry, no problem. I'm off now and will call you when I can return."

"That's fine Andrew. When you do get back and I have things sorted here, we will go up to the hospital to see Winnie Williams."

Harry phoned the police station and spoke to Angela. He gave her the information they had amassed from the CCTV camera and of the attack on Winnie. He asked if she could arrange for Andrew and himself to visit her in the Royal Sussex County hospital later in the day. He also asked her to contact the care home and arrange for a nurse to attend Mary Mills' apartment, number 7, ASAP. She needed help.

"Winnie's apartment is in a dreadful state Angela. We need the fingerprint unit here right away and two uniformed officers. Also could you put me through to Jim in maintenance? I need him to fix Winnie's door with a new lock urgently and install a new phone line connection. That's it thank you Angela. Keep the DCS updated please."

"Of course Harry. I'm just putting you through to maintenance and I will get the uniformed officers and fingerprint team despatched immediately."

"... Hello Jim, Harry here, how are you?"

"Okay thanks. What are you after now?"

"Can you come over now Jim? I will give you the address, it's down by the beach huts at Hove. We called there this morning to interview a lady, the one who discovered the murder victim on the beach. Did you hear about it on the news?"

"Yes Harry, I did. Are you on the case?"

"That's correct. I am working with a new young detective, Andrew Brown. When we arrived here we could see immediately the door had been forcibly broken in and later discovered the telephone wire from the phone to the wall had be cut. The apartment has suffered a good old ransacking Jim. It's in one almighty mess, but I will tell you more when you get here. If you could bring a new lock with a safety chain and a new telephone cable as soon as possible that would be absolutely great."

"No probs Harry, I will be with you in thirty to forty minutes."

"Thanks Jim, see you then."

While Harry was waiting for the police fingerprint team he found a small note book come phone book by the telephone, so took it with him to ask Mary Mills if she knew of any relatives or friends of Winnie's she could phone to inform them of what had happened to her and maybe clear up some of the mess in her apartment.

Mary explained that Winnie had a sister living in Littlehampton, so should she phone her did he think?

"Yes, that would be good. Thank you Mary. If you could ask her to leave it an hour or so though as I see the fingerprint team have just arrived at Winnie's. Oh, and also I have arranged for someone to come in and tend to your foot. They should be here shortly."

"Thank you Sir very much. Thank you so much for caring."

"That's no problem Mary."

Harry went back and explained to the two uniformed police officers and the fingerprint team why they were there. They were all taken aback at how terrible the ordeal must have been for the poor lady, seeing two men in black barge through her home and assault her.

The fingerprint team then painstakingly set about their work on the door and inside the apartment while the two police officers first had a good look around the rear of the building. They wanted to question Mary next but Harry asked them to hold fire for a while as a home care nurse was due to call on her shortly. She was also still badly shaken up at discovering her best friend and neighbour on the floor so ruthlessly beaten up.

"She is making phone calls at the moment too, arranging for Winnie Williams's sister to tidy up this ransacked apartment as soon as the fingerprints team are done."

"Okay Harry, no problem."

Harry thanked them.

Jim soon arrived with his dungaree pockets bulging, a tool bag in one hand and a new door lock in the other.

"Hi Harry. What can you tell me about this job then?"

Harry brought him up to speed.

"Blimey Harry, poor lady, and in her own home too." He shook his head in disgust. "I will just ask the team if I can get this lock changed. I have brought a security chain and the telephone lead as you requested."

"Thanks Jim."

Andrew phoned Harry to confirm everything was now sorted with Tom Wilson. He had explained to Mr Wilson senior why he was concerned for his son, who immediately agreed to stay at home with him for the next five days or however long was necessary. Like everyone else he was appalled at what the thugs had put Winnie through. He certainly did not want the same thing happening to his son.

Andrew then confirmed he had thoroughly searched the area and was completely satisfied there was no sign of anyone resembling the two men they had seen on the CCTV screen.

"That's good news at least Andrew. You can come back here now and we will visit Winnie in hospital."

Just before Andrew returned to the apartments though, Angela phoned Harry with an urgent medical update.

"I'm afraid you won't be able to visit Winnie Harry. I have just received a call from the hospital. She took a turn for the worse and is now in a deep coma."

"Oh no! So very sorry to hear that Angela. Please keep me informed of any further developments."

"I will Harry. What will you do when the team have finished there?"

"Well, they will probably take another hour or so. There's a real mess here to sift through then we will stay on until her sister arrives. First thing in the morning though we will come back down to the coast and commencing with the Best Western hotel thoroughly question all hotels, guest houses, b&bs etc along the front to determine whether the mysterious Mediterranean gentleman had stayed with them at any time. We literally need to check every establishment no matter how small or unlikely in the hope of quickly finding out exactly who he was."

"Very well Harry. I will inform the DCS of the latest situation."

As the fingerprint team had finished in Winnie's apartment they asked if Harry would liaise with the lady next door. They just needed to take her fingerprints for elimination.

"That's fine. I will go and explain to her now."

Harry checked with Mary and yes, she now fully understood that so Harry returned with the team. As they were making their way back a lady came up to Winnie's front door announcing she was Linda Bowman, Winnie's sister.

Harry showed her his identity card, while introducing himself as detective Harry Webb. He explained his assistant Andrew Brown would be arriving soon as originally they had both come to Winnie's apartment to interview her concerning a murder on the beach. As it transpired it was a man who Winnie had both spoken to and later found dead yesterday. She was probably the last person to have conversed with him while he was alive.

Harry explained to Linda what had subsequently occurred to Winnie and that she was now a patient in the

Royal Sussex County hospital. Unfortunately, however, she was not allowed visitors today. Linda was aghast and began to sob.

Harry fetched her a chair and she tried to compose herself. After allowing her a few minutes he asked if she could possibly make a start on tidying up her sister's apartment. Perhaps she could get some help as it would take quite a while? After a little thought she said her husband was working at Haywards Heath and could call in on his way home. He would help her.

Jim gave Linda the two new door keys, explained how the new security catch he had just fitted worked and informed her the telephone line was now reconnected and in full working order.

Linda thanked him but looked a little perplexed. She asked Harry about payment for all the work involved as these sort of things were usually so pricy weren't they? Winnie, she knew was not exactly flush.

"Don't worry Linda, we can cover the cost with our Police Benevolent Community Fund for such cases as these."

"Thank you Sir. Winnie would certainly struggle to pay for the work. We would have needed to club together for her."

Harry smiled at her. He then thanked Jim for coming down so quickly and making such a neat job of the door frame and lock.

"That's just another pint you owe me," he joked.

"Yes, okay, I will try to meet you in the Jolly Tar this weekend."

Andrew arrived back and they both said their cheerio's to Jim. Harry asked Winnie's sister if she would be okay if he and Andrew went back to the police station at that point. She thought it would be as she had just received a text from her husband. Clive was stuck in traffic at the moment but was quite optimistic it wouldn't be for too long.

"Good. Okay we will just make sure Mary next door is comfortable before we leave. Here is my card Linda. Will you please call me anytime if you have any problems?"

Linda nodded appreciatively.

Harry knocked on Mary's door and called out to see if they could come in.

"Yes, please do!"

He asked her how she was and if her foot was more comfortable now. Mary thought it was and was both grateful and impressed with the home care nurse Harry had arranged for her.

"She said she will come in every morning to redress my foot."

Harry smiled, gave her the latest on Winnie's condition and promised to keep her fully informed.

Mary began to weep, crying out, "Poor Winnie, oh, poor Winnie!"

She just could not comprehend why anyone would do that to her friend. "She struggles to get by you know. She is really short of money. Most days she goes down to the beach to help Tom with the deckchairs - at her age too, and it only pays a pittance."

Harry smiled to himself at that little snippet of misinformation and exclaimed, tongue in cheek, "Oh, is that a fact? Well! Here is my card Mary. Please phone me at any time if you have any problems or are worried about anything. Anything at all."

"Thank you Sir. I will."

"What about shopping Mary, is there anyone to help with that?"

"Yes, thank you. We have a friend Colin, in number 2. He has already phoned and offered to do my shopping."

As they left Andrew laughed, "Well Harry, what about that! Mary has absolutely no idea Winnie is walking along the beach most days asking for money. She believes she is helping Tom with the deckchairs!"

"Yes, that was a surprise to me too Andrew. Well, we won't find out anymore until Winnie is out of her coma and back in the recovery ward. It has been a very long day, to put it mildly, so let's get back. What are you doing tonight?"

"I will be in the gym. I have agreed to take a combat training course so that will keep me on my toes!"

"Oh, good for you Andrew! I did all that many moons ago and it is certainly worth the effort. It could save your life one day."

They were soon back. Harry parked up saying, "We will start at 7.30 in the morning. First ports of call all the b&bs and hotels. I will email an account of all today's events to Angela. Cheerio Andrew and good luck tonight."

Andrew arrived just before 7.30 the following morning. Harry was in the car waiting for him so he drove and they set off on the laborious work planned for the day. First hotel was the Best Western. They were armed with a photograph of the Mediterranean gentleman to show receptionists and managers.

Three hours later and absolutely no results.

"Oh drat, but we must persevere Andrew! We are bound to unearth something soon." Harry encouraged.

No sooner had he uttered those words than as if by telepathy the car phone rang. It was Angela.

"Forensics have unearthed a possible room key Harry. Can you both come back to the office now as the DCS wants to discuss this with you."

"We will be with you in fifteen minutes."

"I take it you haven't found out where he stayed yet?"

"No, sorry!"

They arrived at the station precisely thirteen minutes later and headed for the DCS's office.

Angela met them and did a double take - "Gosh you were quick! Did you meet yourselves coming back by any chance?"

"Yes Angela I believe we did you know! Young Sebastian Vettel here Jet propelled us. He thinks he is with Ferrari!" Harry glanced over at Andrew who had reddened slightly.

The DCS asked Angela to stay in his office and thanked her for keeping him updated on Harry and Andrew's reports.

"You are doing a grand job Angela."

"Thank you Sir."

"Now before I show you all what could be a possible room key, I need to tell you Angela rang the hospital this morning. Unfortunately they confirmed Winnie Williams is still in a deep coma. This gentleman concerns me. Her condition is described as critical so if she does not pull through then we will have two murders on our hands.

I was pleased you arranged for Jim our maintenance man to fix the door lock and repair the telephone connection to her home so promptly and I fully support your initiative in arranging for the costs to be paid for by our new Police Benefit Community Fund. She is indeed a worthy recipient. It is good to let the public be made fully aware of how we support anyone who needs the help through no fault of their own.

On to the negative update. We still have no identification for the deceased or for the two men in black you saw on the i360 footage." John Street sighed.

"That is a great shame because it means our investigation is at present stagnant with two suspicious men still on the loose who could, heaven forbid, be highly dangerous to other innocent members of our community. We have to get this thing rolling forward quickly gentlemen please. We have our reputation to think of as well as our duty to the public.

Andrew what is the latest on your news tweet - have they got hold of any additional information yet?"

"I had a ping a few moments ago Sir, I will just check ...

Ah, here we are ... All they say is a local lady by the name of Winnie Williams is in hospital under extremely suspicious circumstances as coincidentally she was the first person to see the murdered man in the deckchair the previous day. They conclude police enquiries are continuing."

"Thank you Andrew. Right, I have in my hand a small plastic spoon shaped item." He held it aloft for them to see. "I am told it could possibly be a room key. It was eventually found by forensics wedged in the toe of one of the deceased man's shoes. The lab have checked it out and confirmed it is electronic."

The DCS passed it over to Harry and Andrew.

"Oh yes," exclaimed Harry "That is most probably a key from The Grand hotel. We held our daughter's wedding there last year and rented rooms. Our key looked similar to this."

"Great, well done Harry! It's best you get onto it right away. See what you can find out. Whatever you do unearth in his room bring every item back here and we will check them out together. This could be the breakthrough we so sorely need."

Chapter 3

Barney Rubble & Sweet Fanny Adams

arry and Andrew were off in a shot. When they arrived at The Grand the concierge directed them to pull up on the right. They produced their ID cards and asked to see the Manager.

The head of concierge was called and said he would take them to see Ms Janice Rawlings. He asked the receptionist to inform her he was bringing up two detectives who needed to speak to her urgently.

They took the elevator to the fourth floor. The concierge knocked on Ms Rawlings door and they entered. Harry introduced himself as the senior detective and Andrew Brown as his assistant detective.

"Thank you Richard, you may leave us now," she nodded politely to the concierge.

Harry explained why they were there and produced the key they had found in the deceased man's shoe. Could she possibly confirm it was one of theirs, he wondered?

"Well yes, it certainly looks as though it is. I will ask someone from reception to come up and check it out on the computer. It won't take too long."

Soon after her call a receptionist knocked on the door and entered. Ms Rawlings asked her to confirm the key was one of theirs and if so to print out details of the guest booked in that room.

Within five minutes the receptionist returned.

"I have a print out for you Ms Rawlings. It certainly is one of our room keys."

The silent sigh of relief coming from within Harry and Andrew was deafening.

"The full name and address is provided on the booking form," she continued, "but unfortunately we have absolutely no details of the occupant's home or mobile numbers. No debit or credit cards were given at the time of booking. Regarding payment, the gentleman booked room number 318 for four consecutive nights and paid in advance in euros. He made no reservations in the car park."

"Thank you Rose. I will call you again if I need you." Ms Rawlings showed them both the booking form:

Name and address:

Mr Dimitris Pantazis
1468 Arios Antonios Nicosia
Cyprus
1011-2865

"I hope that will help you. I am sorry we have no more information. I will take you down to room 318 now and you will be able to inspect it. Maybe you will find something in the drawers or safe to help with your investigation."

"Thank you Ms Rawlings you have been of great help."

As they approached the room Andrew passed cotton gloves to Harry.

"Thanks Andrew."

Ms Rawlings opened the door and they entered. She then drew back the heavy curtains.

Andrew checked the bathroom but there were just the usual hotel toiletries, apart from a bottle of expensive aftershave by Creed - **Men's Adventis.**

Harry checked all the drawers - a Montblanc black rollerball pen, a pair of solid gold cuff links, a silk tie, neatly pressed handkerchiefs and socks.

In the wardrobe hung a few Blake Mill shirts, a smart pair of trousers and a light grey Armani silk suit.

A Louis Vuitton travel case lay on it's side, empty.

Harry studied the safe bolted to the wardrobe floor. It was locked. "Can you get the safe opened for us please Ms Rawlings?"

"Yes, of course. I will call our maintenance man to open it for you. We often get guests who have left the safe locked then forget the code they entered."

The maintenance man duly arrived and opened the safe door for them. Harry quickly put his hand on the door to prevent him from opening it fully. Ms Rawlings thanked the man and after he left the room Harry opened the safe door fully ...

"Haddaway man!" exclaimed Andrew, instinctively slipping into his broadest Geordie accent at what he saw next ...

Harry had pulled out a gun and a round of ammunition. "Giz a deek!" Andrew exclaimed.

"Handle it with care Andrew, it's probably fully loaded."

Andrew emptied it of ammunition - he had used this type of gun recently in training. He placed it carefully on the bed.

Ms Rawlings was horrified. She had never seen a gun before and hadn't expected to see one today, certainly not in her hotel.

Ammunition carefully ejected and the weapon rendered safe, Harry handed Andrew the next item - a Rolex watch. There were some Greek numbers engraved on the back.

Next a photograph of a very attractive young lady in a bright red bikini. She lay elegantly on a lounger under a tree by a blue and white tiled swimming pool. Andrew turned it over. There was some kind of undecipherable inscription and it was signed, *Angie S*.

"Angie S," Andrew exclaimed, "but I can't read the text. It all looks Greek to me!"

"That's because it is Greek Andrew!"

Harry carefully pulled out the next item - "Aha!" He enthused. "Two car keys on an MG ring. Bingo!"

... and that was it.

Harry stood upright and stretched his back, giving it a gentle massage as he did so.

"I need to ask you something important Ms Rawlings. The contents of this safe must not be divulged to anyone. Not to a member of staff, your family, the press ... anyone! "

"Of course Sir."

"Thank you. Now could you please find me a cardboard box and a reel of tape to seal the box before we leave the premises?"

While she was fetching the box and tape Harry asked Andrew to take photographs of the contents, including the writing on the reverse of the photo. They both then pulled out the bed and Andrew stood on a chair to get a better look on top of the wardrobe. There was nothing there.

Ms Rawlings returned with the box and tape and Harry duly sealed it. They all returned to Ms Rawlings' office.

Harry told her he would keep the room key as forensics would need access, also the station would send two uniformed officers soon to pack all the gentleman's belongings into his case and take it away with them to the police station.

"Please don't worry, they will be very discreet. Now, could you please ask the concierge to come up as I would like to ask him about Mr Pantazis's MG car? Also please ask the head waiter to come up. I would like to ask him if Mr Pantazis dined alone that evening or if he had company."

Ms Rawlings made the two phone calls and within minutes Robert the head concierge knocked on her door.

"Robert, detective Harry Webb would like to ask you a question about the car parking."

"Yes, Ms Rawlings."

"Robert, we have just found car keys for an MG car, probably a Classic, maybe a 1960s model at a guess. The room 318 booking is for a Mr Pantazis. I just wondered when he arrived did he ask if his car could be parked in The Grand's car park?"

Andrew showed him the picture they had of Mr Pantazis.

"Yes Sir, I remember he did ask if his MG could be parked for him in our car park. Unfortunately I had to tell him all the spaces were fully booked. He did try to give me a fifty euro note to squeeze his car in but I told him I could not accept money as it was against company policy - and there were certainly no parking spaces."

Ms Rawlings nodded in approval.

"I suggested he go instead to the Brunswick underground car park."

Ms Rawlings thanked Robert with a smile and he left.

Next Gino the head waiter knocked and entered. Ms Rawlings told him the detective wanted to ask him a few questions.

"That's no problem Sir, how can I help you?"

Andrew showed him the photo of Mr Pantazis along with the photo from the safe of the lady in the red dress.

"Gino, we just want to know if you remember this man and if so did he dine in the restaurant alone or was he with this lady?"

"Yes Sir, on two evenings. On the first evening he booked a table for two, ordered a bottle of Moët Chandon Imperial from the sommelier and was joined by a very attractive lady. Could I see the photo again Sir? Ah, yes. That is the lady. She was wearing a low cut black dress and I noticed she wore very bright red shoes.

Mr Pantazis wore a smart light grey suit. They were very friendly and laughed a lot. Mr Pantazis ordered our best fillet steak, the chateaubriand. The lady chose a vegan chickpea, vegetable and apple tagine. They then asked for two Metaxa brandies. Mr Pantazis told me it was his favourite as he was a Greek Cypriot.

When they finished their meal the lady asked me to call her a taxi. Mr Pantazis asked for the bill and paid in euros.

The following evening he was joined in the restaurant by a man constantly arguing with him. The man was extremely smart, wore a cream shirt, steely blue tie and a fitted black suit. His hair was thick and black with a white streak to one side. He had a neatly trimmed beard. They ordered chicken cordon bleu and Keo beers followed by espressos. I believe he was a Greek Cypriot too. Once again Mr Pantazis paid the bill in euros."

Harry was delighted with this detailed information and asked Ms Rawlings if they could have a look at their CCTV in the morning. They wanted to get a picture of the man Mr Pantazis dined with.

"Can I go back to the restaurant now Sir?"

"Yes Gino," Harry said, "Grazie Gino."

Harry and Andrew thanked Ms Rawlings and said they would phone her to see when it would be convenient to view the footage on their CCTV.

As they put the box into the car boot Harry asked Andrew to take it to the DCS's office while he walked along to the Brunswick car park. He would then drive the MG back to the police compound.

"Yes, okay Harry, but could we just go back to the hotel room for a few minutes first? My gut says something is not quite right and I would like to check it out." They both took the lift back up to room 318.

Andrew unlocked the door. He pulled the desk chair over a few yards, stood on it and tried to remove the central heatings air conditioning grill.

"What are you up to Andrew?"

Andrew quickly explained that before he joined the police he worked briefly for a central heating company, fixing grills in numerous hotels and offices. He noticed, when he was looking on top of the wardrobe earlier, the grill wasn't fully closed ... so ... standing on the chair he opened the hatch ... "Oh yes, yes!" (his voice distorted and quietened as his head disappeared) ... then he reappeared triumphantly. "Bingo!" he boomed as he produced a leather case which he handed down to Harry. "Careful, it's heavy," he warned.

Harry placed it on the bed. There were two four digit code locks on the side.

"Well done Andrew! Brilliant detective work," beamed Harry. "When you've replaced the grill will you take this case along with the sealed box back to the office."

Andrew replaced the heating and air conditioning grill and pulled the chair back under the table. He did a celebratory little jump in the air and clicked his ankles together. There was a broad grin on his face as he locked the door and left The Grand hotel.

With the case and the sealed box safely in the car he made his way back to the police station. On the way he sent a radio report detailing the day's events to Angela and asking if she would forward everything on to the DCS to discuss on Harry's arrival.

"Of course Andrew and thank you."

As Harry was looking through the Brunswick car park he saw a few lads aimlessly kicking beer cans and shouting but they soon cleared off as he approached them. He was only there a few minutes when he noticed an MGB in a corner. He took a good look around it. It was a bright red MGB and conveniently parked under a CCTV camera.

The car was in excellent condition and sported a classy black leather interior. Harry unlocked the door, eased himself in, made a small adjustment to the seat and turned the key. Magic! It started like a dream and he wore the most satisfying of smiles as he drove off. It was absolutely brilliant to be driving a red MGB again!

He had a few words with Bob in the police compound and told him why he had brought the car in. He explained he would arrange for forensics to check it over but in the meantime could Bob get one of his mechanics to unscrew the radio and check the wiring ASAP? He was concerned that strangely it was not working and he wondered why as everything else in the car was functioning as sweet as a nut.

"That'll be fine 'arry, no probs."

Before he left Bob he took a photograph of the number plate which he emailed to Angela, asking her to get a full DVLA check.

When he finally arrived at the main office both Andrew and Angela were already there and waiting for him. Angela knocked on the DCS's door and they all trooped in.

"Take a seat please and place the sealed box together with the leather case on the side desk. Andrew, I've just read through your radio report which Angela typed up on today's extraordinary events. Well done both of you!"

Andrew beamed.

"Before we commence any further though, earlier I telephoned the hospital for an update on Winnie Williams's condition. They told me she appears to be making a very slow recovery and they are hopeful she may be out of the coma soon. We may have another problem though ... the chief medical doctor I spoke to informs me there have been numerous complaints of two men who are dressed in black jeans and black jackets hanging around outside the hospital. As a consequence of this I have arranged a 24 hour uniformed police guard."

"That is very worrying Sir," sighed Harry. Andrew agreed.

"Yes, it is. So, when we have finished here Angela could you please phone Winnie's neighbour Mary and her sister Linda - I think I have their names correct - to explain that Winnie is still in a coma but for her safety the hospital will no longer issue any information to anyone over the phone."

Angela nodded.

"So, progress at last! We now know the name of the deceased and that his home is in Cyprus. Right Harry let's now examine what you have just brought in!"

Angela dutifully passed around the white gloves.

"Let's start with the safe. The hand gun and the ammunition. I read that you disarmed it Andrew?"

"Yes Sir. I identified it as a Colt .25 with a silencer. I recently fired one on the shooting range at Hendon."

"Well done Andrew. Very pleased your training came in useful." Andrew nodded appreciatively.

"Then the Rolex watch. It looks extremely expensive and has a series of both letters and numbers engraved on the back. What do you make of them Harry? Any sense?"

"I have a few thoughts on them Sir. I just need to recheck a few things. There are 24 letters in the Greek alphabet. The 'pi' sign is for the mathematical value of 3.142 and 'mu' is micro symbol (u). The engraving on the back is 'u + 03ff. I will get back to you later with the answer. I thought it might be the four digit code for the case."

"Okay Harry. It sounds as though you are on the right track. If anyone can decode it you can," he acknowledged.

"Now, the photo of the lady. It has been confirmed she dined with our man, Mr Pantazis one evening. Any thoughts on where the photo could have been taken?"

"Yes Sir. I am certain it is in Cyprus. The tree she is sitting under is a golden watte, prevalent there, otherwise known as a mimosa in England and if you look beyond her on the left you will see the Troodos mountains."

"Yes, that's probable Harry. My wife and I have been on holiday there. What do you make of the writing on the back?"

"Well, it's very endearing. What she is saying is, 'you are my erastis' meaning 'you are my lover' and 'you are my Melissa' meaning 'you are my honey bee'. 'You are my agape mou' meaning 'my darling' and 'mystikos' is 'our secret'."

"Thank you Harry you're still very good at interpreting. I think I should lock all this in my office safe now before we have a go at getting the leather case opened."

The Superintendent had just closed his safe when there was a loud knock on the door and Bob from the police compound came bounding in.

"Sorry Gov, to bother ya but I think this is very important to yer enquiry! Never seen anything like it I ain't!"

Bob took large strides over to Harry and handed him a small silk bag. "You wus right about the radio 'arry! I decided not to wait for the car maintenance to take it from the MGB but to 'elp you out I removed it meself - with extreme care though so I 'ope I ain't in any Barney Rubble?

There was indeed a loose connection but this small bag wus the culprit! Tip the contents out the bag 'arry!"

"Okay Bob, let's see what you've got here."

Andrew and Angela let out a gasp in unison, "A handful of diamonds. Wow!"

The DCS and Harry both took a few steps nearer to examine the find more closely.

"They are worth a cool £25,000 easily and quadruple that if they are pure!" Harry whispered in disbelief.

Harry asked Bob if he had shown or told anyone else about the diamonds before coming up to them. "Nope. Came straight 'ere."

"That's great Bob and no, you are certainly not in any trouble!"

The superintendent concluded he would keep the jewels under lock and key in his office. This, after all was an ongoing murder case.

"As I have to work strictly within police protocol I have to ask you not to disclose any of this to anyone. I do not want the media or tabloids broadcasting anything we have seen or discussed. I will address them when I feel the time is right."

Harry thanked Bob. "No probs 'arry. I'm pleased I could be of 'elp and you know I won't discuss any info." Bob left the office.

The superintendent asked Angela to lock the office door and close the blinds before they tried opening the case. He didn't want anyone else to come barging in.

"Okay you two, so how are we going to open this then? It's quite heavy - it could be just a couple of bricks inside!"

Harry and Andrew tried a few standard combinations without success.

"Diddly squat!" sighed Andrew, throwing his arms up in despair.

The superintendent threw a long, bewildering glance in Andrew's direction then asked Harry, "Do you think the code is something to do with the numbers on the Rolex?"

"No Sir. I have a feeling that code is for something larger. I will try my special key set Sir."

Harry carefully took a small zipper bag from his shirt pocket and produced a strange metal 'V' shaped object which he slid in the side of the combination lock. He twiddled it methodically and in less than a minute the lock clicked open. He repeated the procedure on the second lock which also clicked open.

"Well," exclaimed the DCS, "I didn't know you could do that Harry! That's a weird phrase and a new trick I have learnt in the last two minutes from you both."

Andrew reddened in the face slightly and Harry replied, "It's not something I would pass on to anyone Sir but it has opened many a door or lock when needed." Harry slowly opened the lid and to everyone's surprise the case was full to the brim with euro notes.

"This must be the money the two men were after when they attacked Winnie Williams. We should count up then put it in the safe with the other items netted today."

The DCS divided the various denominations between them and so began the big count. After a while it was all neatly stacked, all €35,000 of it! Very soon every note was repacked and back in the case.

Angela drew back the blinds and unlocked the door. She then made the two phone calls to Winnie's sister and neighbour then contacted the DVLA for information on the MGB.

The DCS asked Harry and Andrew to discuss future action as there were still many questions that needed answers, like:

1) The deceased man is now known to be Mr Dimitris Pantazis. Good. But why no credit cards, wallet or mobile phone?

2) The two men who attacked Winnie Williams were looking for the case of euros. Good that is now established. They don't know it's here under lock and key and will not stop looking until they find it. It's thanks to Andrew's good thinking that we now have it in our possession. One of them of course murdered Mr Pantazis. Why? Who are they? How did they know he had €35,000? Are they working alone or are they part of a crime syndicate? Do they know about the diamonds in the MGB?

3) Who is the lady in the red dress? We need more information on her.

4) The man in the restaurant arguing with Mr Pantazis - who is he?

"Just one other thing Harry. What made you think something could be hidden behind the car radio?"

"That was just a piece of exceptional good luck Sir. Many years ago I used to own a similar car. A red MGB and it had an exceptional stereo system - all of those cars do so when I turned on the radio in the MGB today and it wasn't working, alarm bells rang. That's why I asked Bob to get it checked out. I'm glad I did!"

"Excellent! What's your next move Harry?"

"Well until we find out more about the MGB Sir, it's back to the laborious task of checking out the CCTV cameras both at the hospital and The Grand's dining room. We might just get lucky and be able to pick up a photo of the two men at the hospital or the man dining with Mr Pantazis. We need to ask the concierge staff if they know where the lady asked the taxi to take her. Was it to the railway station perhaps or to a private address in Brighton?"

"Okay, that's sensible. Keep me informed via Angela, who in turn will call you when she has any leads on the car's registration."

The DCS thought for a moment then added,"I will make a call to the Nicosia police. I happen to know Yiannis Galanis, the chief constable. I'll see what he knows of Mr Pantazis, if anything. I will keep you informed. You may have to go out there in the near future for a few days.

I would like to know more about this mystery man. Was he a resident in the UK for example or just a visitor or business man? If the later, which seems more feasible, we need to establish what his business was here in Brighton and what he does for a living in Cyprus. Is he domicile there?

Well, I think that's all for now gentlemen. Please be vigilant. These two men are, needless to say, highly dangerous!"

"Yes Sir," they both replied in unison.

"We will start with the CCTV camera at the hospital," Harry added.

As they were leaving the superintendent's office there were two loud 'pings!' "Is that your mobile Andrew?"

"Yes Sir I will just check the Brighton news update ... it's saying the lady, Winnie Williams, who discovered the murdered man in the deckchair is still in a coma and the police have a 24 hour guard outside her door. Well, they soon got the info on that didn't they Harry?"

"Let's get over there and find out what's going on."

"Okay Sir, we're on our way."

As they approached the hospital the traffic was gridlocked. Cars were either circling, looking for spaces or queuing to park. Harry suddenly noticed a black Ford with two men inside driving slowly in the opposite direction. "It's them!" He yelled, pointing frantically - at which point the occupants eye balled them and sped off out. Andrew thumped the steering wheel in exasperation.

"Damn and blast it! There's no way I could turn Harry! I'm absolutely gutted."

Dejected they eventually parked up and went into reception. After showing their ID cards they asked if they could speak to the head medical doctor. Also, later they would like to speak to the maintenance manager or whoever was in charge of the CCTV cameras at the front of the hospital.

After a few minutes Mr Kapoor came down to reception and on seeing their ID cards asked Harry and Andrew to come up to his office.

On the way up in the lift Andrew nudged Harry then whispered quietly, "He's not a happy bunny. I think something is wrong ..."

The lift stopped at level 9 and they followed him into his office. Mr Kapoor asked them to take a seat.

"I'm afraid the news is bad. Sadly Winnie Williams has passed away. My staff did everything possible to save her. She came out of her coma in the middle of the night and slowly began to regain consciousness. Unfortunately though she then suffered a massive heart attack. Despite staff giving her full CPR they could not restart her heart. I was just about to telephone your DCS to explain this when you arrived."

Harry and Andrew were both visibly shocked and saddened by the news. This confirmed of course they were now dealing with two murders.

"Should I still phone your DCS?" asked Mr Kapoor.

"Yes please," advised Harry, "as he may still want to discuss this deeper with you. I would like to have a word with the police officer on guard here, ask him to stand down and return to the station. I will then contact Mrs Linda Bowman, Winnie's sister in Littlehampton. Thank you doctor."

Harry and Andrew went to the ward and found the police officer outside the side room door. Harry knew him.

"Hi John, have you been updated on the latest here?"

"Not exactly Harry. Everyone has gone quiet as the grave here now after one hell of a commotion an hour ago but no one has filled me in."

Harry explained how Winnie had died.

"I thought that was it but I wasn't told officially. Should I return to the station?"

"Yes John and thanks. Could you tell planning that no other officers will be required here?"

John nodded. "I'll see you later."

"Right Andrew, sadly we now have two murders on our hands. One step forward, two steps back - we are being led a merry old dance! Right, let's ask if we can view the CCTV cameras here. We might just strike lucky and get the registration number of that black Ford."

They asked in reception to see the maintenance manager.

"Of course. I will give Jamie a call for you."

After a few minutes an amiable young man appeared. They showed their ID cards, explained their business and Jamie asked them to follow him to the office.

Harry explained what they were looking for as Jamie rolled the footage back.

"So, what is the make and colour of the car?"

"A black Ford. We couldn't get the registration but are quite certain there were two men inside."

"Oh yes! I have seen that car hanging around here lately too Sir. Just give me 30 minutes tops and I will scroll through the last few days filming. In the meantime make yourselves comfy next door and I will arrange for coffee to be brought to you."

After about 25 minutes they heard Jamie call out to them so they returned to his office.

"Great! Got it Sir! Have a close look at this … I'm sure that's the one - a black Ford with two male occupants. I will make a blow up print for you which will enable you to read the number plate."

"Thanks Jamie. Thank you very much."

"No problem Sir I am pleased to be of help. Let me know if you need any more prints."

As they were leaving the hospital Andrew commented, "Let's hope we can get a trace on the Ford's plate, it will be the breakthrough of the day."

His phone rang. It was Angela Jones. "We have information on the MGB. It was registered to a garage near Haywards Heath who specialise in classic cars. It was hired out to Mr Dimitris Pantazis and the garage owner gave the address we already hold for him in Nicosia, Cyprus. He paid for the rental in euros.

The owner asked if the car could be collected from us and he became really stroppy when I told him no it couldn't as it was needed here as evidence in a murder investigation and would have to remain here in the police compound for as long as it took.

I will forward the garage address to you. The DCS wants you to see just how easy it is to hire a classic car for cash. The manager is a Mr Max Grey. The DCS is also concerned perhaps other cars at this garage may also have a little package behind their radios!"

"Okay Angela. Understood. Leave it with us."

"We also had a phone call from Mr Kapoor at the hospital. He informed us of Winnie's tragic death, after coming out of the coma at one point too. So sad!"

"Yes, it is very upsetting. I will update Harry on the classic car garage and we will go over to Haywards Heath now. Before you go though Angela, just one more thing. We have a registration number for the black Ford! I will text it to you now - see if you can trace it please. I will be surprised if the plates are genuine though - more likely to be stolen!"

"That's great Andrew, thanks. I will get back to you soon."

Harry logged the garage's postcode into the sat-nav. It was between Haywards Heath and Gatwick.

Andrew asked how they should approach the owner, being as he had such an aggressive manner.

"Good question Andrew," Harry acknowledged. "I think we should be polite but firm - and ask for all the keys to every MGB he has on the premises. We will look under their bonnets, in their car boots and when I get the chance I will sit behind their wheels and turn their radios on."

"He won't like it! What will you do if you find one with a faulty radio?"

"Drive it back to the compound!"

Andrew winced. He could foresee an argument brewing.

As they approached the garage they saw a few MGBs outside. They parked up and went in.

A sharply dressed man came out and asked if they were the police detectives from Brighton. Harry and Andrew both nodded as they produced their ID cards.

The man was not friendly and he thrust his business card towards them. "I'm Max Grey the manager/owner here. I want to know just exactly what you are doing and why you think you have the right to keep my red MGB in your police compound? I demand it back now! Pronto!"

"I am sorry Mr Grey but that is just not possible as I believe you were informed by our DCS earlier."

Max scowled at Harry.

Unperturbed Harry continued, "What other MGBs do you have besides those on your forecourt?"

"They are the only ones at the moment. One white, two green and one black."

"What can you tell us about Mr Pantazis, the man who hired the car from you?"

"Okay, he always has that particular car when he comes over from Cyprus. Yes, always he does. We take it over to Gatwick for him to pick up on his arrival then zoom, he's gone!"

"Do you have a UK address for him, or a mobile number or perhaps an email address?"

"No. I don't have any UK numbers only the one landline in Cyprus. He never gives us any addresses or tells us where he stays while he is here. He just said he moves around a lot and only stays in hotels."

"How does he pay?"

"He always pays in euros. Only ever euros. Look, I need that MGB back soon. I have another customer from Cyprus wanting to hire it and no other car will do!"

"Oh, interesting! Can you give us the two Cyprus numbers you are holding please?"

"Do I have to?" he snarled, walking angrily round in a circle like a caged lion.

"Well, let's put it like this Mr Grey, if you won't cooperate here and give us the information we require then we will be left with absolutely no option but to take you back with us to Brighton police station for questioning and I really don't want to do that."

"Okay, okay. The other guy from Cyprus is a Mr Nico Castellanos. He was due to arrive in Gatwick this week but phoned me yesterday and postponed his arrival to a fortnight from now. I will look up the phone numbers."

"Thank you Max. Now, can we have the keys to the four MGBs on your forecourt please?"

"No most definitely not! Are you taking the p i - -? I'm not letting you! How on earth can they be part of your investigation?"

"Well Max let me explain again. The alternative is that we call our DCS now, to get a search warrant issued. He will then send a police search team here directly to thoroughly search your entire premises, leaving absolutely nothing unturned and will probably take all your accounts away for close inspection to boot! It's entirely up to you ... ?"

"Okay, okay. You win. I will get the four sets of keys for you." He marched angrily inside and returned dangling the keys on his forefinger. "Here you are and make sure you don't put so much as a scratch on them or I will see to it you pay for any repairs!"

"Yes Max. We will be careful." Harry assured him.

"Right Andrew, let's get started with the two green ones."

After about fifteen minutes they had completed thorough checks on both cars, under their bonnets, under carpets, in their boots and their radio systems. Nothing!

"Okay Andrew - the black one next."

Same there, "Absolutely diddly squat!" sighed Andrew.

"Right ... just this white one then."

And all was looking fruitless with that too until Harry turned on the radio ... Zilch!

"Right! This is coming back to the compound with us. Let's give Max the news - he won't be a happy bunny!"

They walked into his office. "Max. We are taking the white MGB back with us for further investigation."

"NO! WHAT? Oh no please, you can't do that, you just can't! You'll ruin me! You'll absolutely ruin me!"

"Okay Max. I will phone the DCS who will send a transporter to collect it and they won't be as careful as us."

"Alright, alright. You had better take it but you make sure it isn't damaged! Do you hear me? I do have a business I'm trying to run here you know!"

"Good. Now, can I double check with you Max. You said you had no more MGBs on the premises but do you perhaps have any others out on hire to customers by any chance?"

"Yep. There are two blues and one green out on hire at present. That's the lot."

"Okay, just before we go Max, take a look on Andrew's phone at a black Ford car. Have you seen it around here?"

Andrew showed Max the photo.

"Yes, I have as a matter of fact," enthused Max, "with two men inside. They didn't come into the garage but I thought they looked a tad suspicious. Who are they then? Are they the reason I am being persecuted here?"

"Well, if you see this car here again call us immediately. Do not approach them though - they are dangerous!"

"I will. I will. I don't want any trouble."

"Okay, we will go now and I will drive the MGB. Don't worry I used to own one and it was my pride and joy. Here are your other car keys."

Harry led the way and Andrew followed. As they arrived at the station Harry drove the car straight into the compound.

" 'ello 'arry, you 'ere again are ya? What you doin' me old cocker, collecting MGBs then?"

"Yes Bob. I found another one with a faulty radio. Come up to the DCS's office if you discover anything."

"Okay 'arry I'll get on it right away!"

Harry and Andrew went up to the DCS's office. They discussed the events at the garage and how Max Grey had been so obstreperous initially then mellowed somewhat after hearing the alternatives put to him.

"I don't think he wanted us to see his accounts!" laughed Harry, "I think he has money troubles at the moment!"

Just then Angela knocked and entered, "I have received some information on the black Ford Sir. You were right to suspect the number plates were stolen. The car is actually registered to a bus company in North Wales for - wait for it - a bright orange double decker bus!"

"Thank you Angela," the DCS chuckled. "Would you circulate this information to all units ASAP. Highlight the fact it is an urgent murder case and to keep well back if they do spot the car as the two men inside are highly dangerous and likely to be armed."

"Yes Sir. I will do that now."

Harry then explained to the DCS about the other Cypriot, Mr Nico Castellanos, who wanted to be picked up from Gatwick to specifically hire the very same MGB Mr Dimitris Pantazis had hired. Highly suspicious!

"My guess is he must be in contact with the two men in the black Ford who would by now have informed him the MGB is now in the police compound. That's why he postponed his flight from Cyprus. Will you be discussing this with Mr Galanis the police chief in Nicosia Sir?"

"Yes, I most certainly will Harry. In fact I will call him just as soon as we have finished here."

Bob knocked on the DCS's door.

"Come in Bob. Did you find anything in the white MGB?" he asked.

"Yep Gov! I did. A small bag of sparklers. Make some lovely Tom Foolery them would!"

"I must ask you once again to keep this confidential Bob."

"Of course Gov. No probs! I will go now, put the radio back in and make sure it's in full working order."

"Great, that's fine. Please call me when both cars are ready and I will get the garage to collect them," instructed the DCS.

Bob doffed an invisible cap as he took his leave.

"Well, Harry and Andrew, what do you plan next now we have even more diamonds in our safe?"

"I'm hoping we will get reports of a further sighting on the Ford very soon Sir. We do need more information on the diamonds though, like who's putting them behind the radios and who collects them," pondered Harry, perplexed ...

"Just why are they stowed specifically in the MGBs from Mr Grey's garage and is he involved in any of this? Why too do some of those Cypriot names sound so familiar? ... Oh! Hold on, I've just remembered. I picked up a small note book containing telephone numbers and a few addresses from Winnie Williams' apartment when we were sorting through her trashed flat. I'll fetch it." Harry disappeared for a minute or two.

"Here it is, let's have a look through ... Oh Wow! Yes! Look at this - we have a telephone number for Mr Pantazis in Cyprus."

"So she knew him?"

"Yes, no wonder she was so hysterical on the beach! The other numbers are mostly just local - her neighbours, her sister in Littlehampton, also, let me see ..."

He flipped over a couple of pages, "ummm, just a taxi firm and her hairdresser. That's it. But Mr Pantazis eh? Strange ..."

"So why was she beaten up? Because of a connection with Mr Pantazis or because she was suspected of having the euros? And why was Mr Pantazis murdered on our beach?"

"I don't know. This whole case is becoming more and more complex Sir. Her knowing Mr Pantazis has put a whole new spin on things though."

"Indeed. Do you have any more reports on your news feed app Andrew?"

"Nothing new Sir. They just say the police are still investigating the murder on Brighton beach and reporting the death of Winnie Williams at the Royal Sussex hospital. There is no mention of the MGBs."

"That's good Andrew, thank you. Keep me informed of any updates as soon as they occur."

"Yes, of course Sir."

Just as Harry and Andrew were leaving, Bob rang the DCS and reported both MGBs were ready to be returned to the garage at Haywards Heath.

"Thanks Bob, I will ring Mr Grey and ask him to pick them up." It was the DCS's turn to look momentarily pensive, then he turned to Harry.

"I will let you know when they are to be collected. I think you should follow at a distance, just to see where they are taken. Perhaps it is all hot air with Mr Max Grey but I need to know for sure."

"Yes Sir."

Angela then knocked and entered. "Sorry to bother you Sir but Max Grey is on the line and demanding to speak to you personally."

"That's okay Angela, put him through. Stay here Harry and Andrew. Let's see what he wants." Harry and Andrew took a few steps back and listened with interest as the phone was put onto loudspeaker.

"Hello Mr Grey. DCS Street here. How can I be of assistance?"

"I want my two MGB cars returned. I need them now! I have customers waiting to hire them and there you are not giving a tinker's cuss and costing me thousands to boot!"

"Calm down Mr Grey. I have just this minute got the clearance on both cars and they await your collection?"

"What! *My* collection? Won't *you* bring them back to my garage?"

"No, afraid not Mr Grey. You will have to come to our Brighton compound to collect them and sign the necessary paperwork."

"Oh I don't believe you lot! Okay, I will send two of my drivers down now. Those cars had better not be damaged in any way though or you will be given the bill to put them right!" at that the phone was slammed down.

"Well Harry and Andrew, you heard the man. As charming as a septic verruca isn't he? Please follow discreetly."

"Yes Sir and we'll keep you informed."

"Come on Andrew, let's go down to the compound and have a coffee with Bob before the drivers arrive."

Within forty minutes the two cars had been collected and driven away. Harry and Andrew followed at a safe distance. They were taken straight to the Classic garage though where My Grey met them, gave both cars a cursory check over then drove them into the showroom.

"Well, that all looks innocent enough Harry. What next? Do you think the DCS wants us to hang on here?"

"No, might as well go back now and see what tomorrow brings. You had better just update the DCS though Andrew."

Next morning as DCS John Street arrived and made his way up to the office Angela Jones came running in after him.

"Sir, I have just received a call from the hospital. There was a major incident overnight. Mr Max Grey has been shot and is now in the recovery ward."

"What! When?"

"Apparently in the early hours Sir, following an intruder alarm call to his mobile. That's all I know."

"Right get Andrew and Harry to go to the garage at Haywards Heath now - see if they can get any more info on exactly what is going on. It's got to be those same two men again in the black Ford. Why on earth hasn't that car been picked up yet? It's on alert in every ruddy police car and in every station all over the country for heaven's sake,"

"I know Sir. They appear to be the ghosts of Houdini! But we will get them soon and they will both pay dearly for all this."

"I certainly hope so Angela. If you would please ring the hospital in about an hour's time I would like to speak to someone in the recovery ward."

While driving towards the garage Harry and Andrew pondered various scenarios. Harry wondered if the men in the black Ford could have been watching when the MGBs were taken and subsequently returned to the garage.

"Spooky if they had been! ... Yet they were not spotted ... We had warned Max Grey to be extra vigilant regarding that car ... Bewildering! More than bewildering - even Confucius would be tongue tied and pulling out his hair!" Harry sighed.

"Did he even have hair Harry?"

"I think so. Wasn't it him who thought it barbarous to cut hair?"

Andrew shrugged.

As they arrived at the garage they noticed blue police tape crossing the entrance and two police cars were parked up. Harry and Andrew flashed their ID cards at the officers on the scene.

"Alright chaps? We will take over now. We were here yesterday."

"Yes Harry. We have all the information from your DCS. He did call giving us a brief outline."

"That's good. Any sightings of the black Ford yet?"

"No Harry, sorry. We are all on alert though to call DCS John Street if we do."

"Okay. So what can you tell us of the events during the early hours this morning?"

"All we know so far is Mr Grey had a direct alarm line to his mobile in the event of any break ins or disturbances at the garage.

He lives about four miles away and his wife confirmed he had a warning alert on his mobile about 5am. He immediately dressed and sped straight here. On arrival he saw two men searching through some of his cars. He tried to stop them but they brandished guns and shouted something about missing diamonds.

He yelled back that he didn't have a clue what they were talking about and as he was about to ring 999 they shot him. Luckily the bullet hit him in the shoulder but he stayed down, feigned death so they presumed they had killed him and drove off. He managed to ring us so we arranged for an ambulance to take him to the Royal Sussex. We then phoned his wife, Jane.

She called in here briefly before driving to the hospital and as far as we know she is still there.

We advised the mechanics to contact their recent customers to explain due to circumstances beyond their control they would have to close the garage temporarily."

"Okay. Who are the mechanics?"

"One is off sick so just two turned up for work today and they are both out the back. Do you want to question them?"

"Certainly. All is not as it should be with this garage."

"Okay Harry, we will leave you to it! Their names are Alex Bennet and Stan Knibbs. They both seem really amiable."

"Thanks. We will have a word with them now."

Harry and Andrew introduced themselves to Alex and Stan and explained they would have to ask a few questions. They both nodded in agreement and Harry began:

"Do you maintain and repair all the Classic cars here?"

"We are responsible for all the maintenance with the exception of any electrical work, for example the radios and the interior lighting."

"Oh, that's interesting," exclaimed Harry. "Does that apply to just the MGBs or others like the Citroen DS23 Pallas you have in the showroom?"

"Yes Sir all the classics go away to be rewired if required. You have a very good knowledge of the classics Sir."

"Yes, I admit to having an extremely keen interest in the classics to the extent my friends always referred to me as 'a geek'. I'm particularly fond of the MGBs and the Citroens as I drove them during my Halcyon days. Tell me about the radios though. Are they a special type?"

"Yes Sir they are top of the range with a 6 speaker surround sound. We take the cars to a unit at the rear of Gatwick airport to fit them."

"Are any of the cars there now?"

"Most cars are here with the exception of two black Citroens and 3 MGBs out on hire."

"Thanks very much for your help. Could you tell me the address of the unit at Gatwick please?"

"Yes, of course Sir. It's easy to find: Unit 11, Airport Road, North Terminal, Gatwick."

"Okay - but could you give other more specific details you may hold in your records; postcode, phone numbers etc to detective Brown here. Do you know how many work there?"

"We have only seen two lads, both in their 30s I should think."

"Just one more question, how do you get on with Mr Grey?"

"He's a good boss Sir. We have both worked here for the last two years."

"Has he ever had trouble paying your wages?"

"No. Not until recently that is. He was a bit late in paying but I don't know why for sure. It was rumoured though that he lost a few games of poker."

"Thank you Stan and Alex for your honest replies."

"What about the busted lock Sir?" Stan asked.

"Just check it out with the local police - I see forensics are here now. If they give the okay call a 24 hour repair firm then ask Mr or Mrs Grey to contact the garage's insurance company."

"Thanks Sir. I will go over to ask the police now."

Harry asked Andrew to drive as he wanted to email Angela a full updated report to pass on to the DCS.

"Okay Harry. You certainly know how to ask the right questions. I am learning bucket loads just by accompanying you."

"Yes, a few years of experience helps Andrew and sometimes just an innocuous question asked in the right manner will yield a fruitful outcome. Never bully a response - be their confidant."

Andrew found the industrial units quite easily and drove straight up to number 11. It was closed and protected by roll up doors with double security locks. The name on the door was 'Surround Sound Systems'.

"Right Andrew, let's have a good look around and establish just what goes on in here. It looks as though unit 12 is closed and 10 is a printing firm. Lots of other units are closed too. The place is semi derelict. You go into 10, the printing firm and ask the relevant questions while I check out the back here."

"Okay Harry." Andrew knocked, walked in and showed his ID. "I need to ask you about Surround Sound Systems next door."

"I may be able to help you. What would you like to know?" asked what looked like the man in charge.

"Thanks. Firstly how well do you know the two men who work next door?"

"Only briefly. I would have a few casual words with one of them like out the back over a coffee."

"Do they normally come here every day?"

"Oh no! Only twice, maybe three times a week like."

"How long have they been here?"

"Only a few months. They just had the odd classic car in. On occasion, if they hadn't finished work on a car like they would keep it locked up here overnight."

"Could you tell me who owns these units?"

"A man from the East End. I don't have any info on him like but I should think you could find out quite easily. He has been pushing up the rental charges here recently. That's probably why next door left. One of them did say they were well behind with the rent like."

"What vehicle did the two lads drive?"

"A white Ford Transit van and last night they loaded all their equipment, the whole blooming kit and caboodle like, into the van and waved goodbye. Sweet Fanny Adams left in there and Sweet Fanny Adams chance of them ever returning I'd say."

"Did you ever see anyone visiting the unit?"

"Yes, once or twice a month a man in a silver blue Audi would park up outside. You could hear them talking like and sometimes him shouting quite aggressively."

"Could you give me a description of the man?"

"Yep! He was quite smartly dressed, dark haired with a white streak to one side. He had a neat little beard like and a well fitted black suit with a white folded hanky in the breast pocket. Very distinguished he was."

"Thank you for the detailed information. I didn't catch your name?"

"Oh, I'm Ted Jones. I have worked here for about four years. If you need to know anything else like mate, anything at all just call me on this number." He produced a business card.

"Thanks Ted I will."

"One more thing I forgot to say though mate is the CCTV camera is kaput this end. It looks as though the one on the end of unit 12 has been shot out. The one on unit 1 is still working like but it don't reach this far along."

Andrew thanked him again then wandered round the back to look for Harry. Surprisingly he found him inside the unit looking at posters on the wall.

"Was the door left open then Harry?"

"Well ... not exactly ... ," Harry retorted.

Andrew looked over at him questioningly.

"One of my keys did the trick though!" he chuckled. "How did you get on questioning next door?"

"Sweet Fanny Adams like!" Andrew chucked back.

"What?"

"I will explain later, but on a more serious note, yes I got on well. Something of significance came to light too. You remember the man who was dining and arguing with Mr Pantazis in the hotel restaurant who had a white streak in his hair?"

Harry was all ears.

"Well, he was here arguing with the two men working on the cars. I reckon he was the boss who came in to pay them - only thing was there was probably no money to pay them with! Ted from the printing firm next door thought they were behind with their rent too. I will update you fully on the way back and also email Angela.

This place is a bit of a mess isn't it? I will show you the security camera on the way out. Ted thinks someone has fired a bullet through it."

Andrew took a cursory glance around the empty unit. "Nice car posters. Do you know the various models Harry? I recognise the MGB of course. I expect they are mega expensive."

"Yes Andrew. The red MGB there is about £10,000; the Citroen DS23 Pallas, like the one in the garage about £12,000; the Porsche 944.30 about £20,000 and the Jaguar 3.8 E type Coupe about £25,000. So which one floats your boat Andrew?"

"Without doubt the Jag Harry."

"Good choice," Harry smiled back.

"Well, let's get this door locked and have a look at the CCTV camera before we make our way back to Brighton. Daydreaming over for today!"

Harry locked the door with his special key as Andrew looked on in amazement. His aim was to emulate this man one day.

They wandered over to the CCTV. It certainly looked like a bullet hole going straight through the middle.

"Well, I've never seen anything of the sort before Andrew. Okay, I will drive us back while you email Angela."

Andrew had no longer sent the email when Angela rang back to say the DCS was holding a special meeting the following morning at 8 o'clock.

Chapter 4

Diddly Squat

The DCS looked agitated at the start of the meeting. "I'm very concerned we can't locate this darned black Ford and the two armed men inside it! We are throwing everything at this - resources, men - but it and they seem to have vanished into thin air! So, let's start with what we know so far ... what we believe these two are responsible for ...

Mr Pantazis is killed by a single shot through the heart on our beach. A few days later Mr Grey was shot in the shoulder outside his garage and is extremely lucky to be alive. By the way, forensics have just confirmed both men were shot by the same gun.

Then the merciless killing of Winnie Williams. How on earth did she get mixed up in all of this? Was her only 'crime' finding the body? Same two men responsible!

We have recovered €35,000 thanks to Andrew; two small bags of diamonds from the two MGBs, a gun, ammunition, and a Rolex thanks to Harry.

From your visit to Gatwick yesterday," he glanced over at Harry and Andrew, "we know where the MGBs had their radios fitted, but, those who fitted them seem to have 'done a runner' and we know nothing of their identity - diddly squat, to coin that well known phrase!"

Andrew reddened in the cheeks.

"I have contacted the Metropolitan police and explained we need to know pretty darned sharpish who owns those units at Gatwick. They have promised to make it priority.

I have also contacted Yiannis Galanis the police chief in Nicosia. He has been making enquiries about Nico Castellanos trying to establish why he did not take his flight to Gatwick. I am waiting to hear back on that one.

Now Harry, you will need to interview Max Grey as soon as he recovers sufficiently. There may be a lot more he can fill us in on. Agreed?"

"Yes Sir, you are right. He could be being blackmailed." volunteered Harry, Andrew nodded in agreement.

"And of course we still need to glean more information regarding the lady in the photo and the man arguing with Mr Pantazis in the restaurant. Thanks to Andrew we now know he visited the units at Gatwick - so some of the pieces of the puzzle are there - they just need pressing firmly into place not left floating in the ether!"

Angela's desk phone rang so she excused herself to answer it. She was soon buzzing the DCS ... "This is an urgent call for you Sir. It's a police constable from Thames Valley. He is in the North Terminal car park at Gatwick."

"Put him through Angela."

He engaged the loudspeaker. "DCS Street here. What can you tell me?"

"I have some news for you Sir on the missing black Ford car we have on our radar. My name is Chris Collins, I'm with my family flying to Spain today from Gatwick. We have just pulled into the North Terminal carpark, level 4 and as we went to the lift I noticed the black Ford parked in a corner. I have checked the doors and boot but it's securely locked. What I can do, if you require Sir, is ask one of the Gatwick police to come to level 4 and stay by the car until your men arrive?"

"Brilliant! Thank you Chris for phoning me. If you could ask the Gatwick police to guard the vehicle until my team get there that would be great! You have been very alert - well done! Thank you so much for phoning in and enjoy your holiday. You deserve it."

"Okay Harry and Andrew! Our prayers have been answered! Go straight to Gatwick now and check out the car. I will send a transporter from the compound to bring it back here. You will of course need to start it to get it down to ground level."

Andrew's face lit up, "Harry can start it Sir with his special keys!"

"Yes, I can," laughed Harry. "We will go to Departures when the car has been safely picked up. I'm certain those two men are now well on their way to Cyprus."

"I do believe you're right - if so try to get hold of their addresses over there."

"Come on Andrew," urged Harry, "let's go!"

Andrew drove. "Cyprus has been mentioned so much, do you think we will be asked to go there?"

"I'm so sure Andrew I'm even willing to trade hairdressers with you for a one-off cut next month!"

Andrew looked horrified. "Nee! Nee! Nee!" Divent Dee that man!" he begged as he held a hand protectively over his hair.

They arrived at Gatwick's North Terminal and soon came across the black Ford in the corner on level 4 of the carpark being guarded religiously by a uniformed police officer. They showed him their ID cards and explained they had just driven up from Brighton and a transporter would be arriving shortly to pick the car up.

"Okay Sir, that's fine by me. I will leave you to it."

"Thanks for staying with this vehicle," Harry smiled.

Elated to at last have it in their clutches they both took a look round the black Ford. Inside were some discarded old drinks cups and takeaway food cartons. It was in a right mess. Andrew tried the boot and doors but as the officer who found it had said - it was securely locked.

Andrew looked quizzically over to Harry who winked at him and with a deft flourish produced his special keys. A magician's slight of hand would not compare with such dexterity.

Harry smiled at Andrew but warned him it was a fairly new model with a recent electronic push button ...

"... I have managed to open one before though with a combination of my phone and these keys. Just give me a few minutes to fiddle ... CLICK!"

"Brilliant Harry," admired Andrew as all the doors sprang open. "I knew you'd crack it - but how are you going to start it without a key?"

"Okay doubting Thomas, one thing at a time! Open the bonnet ... I'll just check the wiring ... Now, keep it out of gear Andrew and when I say, press the accelerator ... Got it! Now, gently try it."

"Great! It's going Harry! Shall I drive it out?"

"You bet! Take it down and park outside. I will follow on behind - we might have trouble getting through the barrier though but if there is a problem I will sort it."

As they reached the barrier a security guard was there on duty. Harry flashed his ID card. The guard eyeballed them suspiciously but released the barrier and they drove out.

The transporter hadn't yet arrived. "Just stay on the roadside. I will park behind you and put the cones around. Let's have a look in the boot ...

"WOW, look at this Andrew!" Two guns and three rounds of ammunition lay there. "We had better lock these in my boot!"

Andrew looked down at the guns, "Yes, they are .25 Colts with silencers just like the one that shot Mr Pantazis and Mr Grey."

About thirty five minutes later the transporter arrived, pulling up in front of the Ford.

"Thanks for getting it down from level 4 Harry. We'd have created one almighty jam going up in this," jested the driver. "Just show me how you started her up though and I will load her safely onto the transporter."

"Okay. Take a look here. Just touch these two wires together ... see?"

"Just let me try ... okay, got it! I will drive her on and strap her down."

"Give the DCS a call Andrew and tell him we'll soon be on our way. Oh, and tell him we have two guns and ammunition but first we are going over to check out Departures. I know there's a car parking area for police just around the side. Look out for departures to Cyprus I will meet you there."

"Do you think they boarded a flight to Cyprus then?"

"Definitely. Do you fancy that bet now?"

Andrew took two steps back, running his fingers through his hair protectively and went in search of departures for Easy Jet Flights to Larnaca, Cyprus. When he looked round Harry was there beside him.

"Okay Andrew, let's see what we can find out."

They showed their ID to the clerk on the desk and explained this was urgent police business. They needed to know the names of two men who boarded the flight to Larnaca yesterday. Possibly a late booking.

"Yes Sir, I will call the superintendent."

After a few minutes a smartly dressed woman approached them. "Hello, my name is Elaine and I am the Easy Jet superintendent. If you would like to follow me I will take you to the office. I understand you need to look at names on the departures list to Larnaca yesterday?"

"Please," Harry responded.

They soon reached the office and followed Elaine in. "Right, yesterday we had just the one flight to Larnaca at 3.30pm." She scrolled adeptly through pages and pages of text then announced, "Right, here is the list. It just includes a few late bookings so this shouldn't take long gentlemen... Ah here we are, a family of four, a lady travelling alone and look ... two men seated together!"

"That's great Elaine. Can we have all the details you hold for them please? Names, addresses, mobile numbers?"

Elaine scrolled again. "Yes, just bringing up another list now ...ah! This is the one," Elaine smiled at them. "Mr Yirgos Papadopoulos. He gave his address in Nicosia, Cyprus. The second man is Andreas Athanasiou. He gave his address in Palmers Green, London. I believe that area has a large Greek population. I will print this off for you along with their phone numbers."

"Thank you Elaine, you have been a great help."

"No problem Sir. We always like to help when we can. Here you are, the printer has obligingly churned these out for you."

"Great that's just what we needed."

Elaine opened the door for them. "Okay Andrew, let's go. You drive I need a little thinking time."

"Well Harry, you certainly knew how to get the Ford's doors open. How do you know so much?" Andrew marvelled.

"Years of experience Andrew, just years of experience." he smiled.

"I will pass on the details we have just been given to Angela. The DCS will probably call his contact in Nicosia ASAP and the police station at Palmers Green. We'll catch up with the pair of them before long!"

A few minutes later Angela rang. "Hello you two. Brilliant work! I have given your reports to the DCS. He has been called to an urgent meeting but when you get back he has requested you take both guns and the ammunition straight to forensics for fingerprinting and ask them to take everything to the armoury when they have finished.

He wants me to take the gun and ammunition down there from our safe as well.

I have to contact the police at Palmers Green to glean what they know about Mr Andreas Athanasiou then phone Mr Yiannis Galanis at Nicosia police station to request he makes checks on Mr Virgos Papadopoulos and Mr Andreas Athanasiou.

Finally he added you two have done enough this week so after you have deposited the guns at forensics take a break and resume here at 8am on Monday.

... oh, also we received a call from Winnie's sister, Linda Bowman. Winnie's funeral is to be held next Tuesday and he would like you both to attend. It is at Littlehampton Crematorium. I will text you the postcode and the time."

"Thanks Angela. Yes, of course we will go. I would like to have a few words with Linda's husband. I think he works at Haywards Heath and I would like to know just where. You have a break too Angela and see you on Monday."

Harry turned to Andrew, "What are you doing over the weekend young man?"

"Well, I have my combat training course. I will visit the gym, go for a run and then take a rest. Do you think I should get a few books from the library on Cyprus? I have never been there and know diddly squat about the island."

"Good idea Andrew! It would give you a flavour of the place if we are called to go there soon."

"I also need a haircut before we go."

Harry glanced surreptitiously at Andrew. His dark auburn hair was already cut so short you could see his scalp and he was so ultra protective of it ... he certainly did not want to exchange styles in the bet earlier!

"So, what do you call your cut exactly Andrew? What do you ask the barber for?"

"Barber? I don't go to a barber Harry! It's a salon and I ask Celine, my stylist, who smells delicious by the way, for an under cut with buzzed sides. I used to have faded sides but I prefer it now just that tad shorter."

Totally bemused by now Harry studied the style more closely. He hadn't fully understood a word Andrew had just spoken.

In turn Andrew looked over at Harry's black hair that was just slightly greying in a place or two. It was too long, through his eyes, but neatly cut and quite distinguished.

"So, what do you ask your barber for then Harry?"

Harry thought for a moment then replied, "'The usual'. Everyone who goes in asks Arthur for 'the usual' ... and before you ask he smells of stale smoke and Brylcreem!"

After a short silence they both let out hearty laughs, accepting their differences graciously.

"So what are you doing this weekend then Harry?"

"Well, I will probably tidy up the garden then go for a pint with Bob and Jim. I owe them both a drink. We will go to the Jolly Tar and watch the match on the big screen. Then on Sunday I might take the wife out for lunch. Tell you what, give me a call on Sunday morning and maybe you could join us? She would like to meet you."

"Thanks Harry I would like that too."

On Sunday morning Andrew gave Harry a ring. "Is it still okay for me to join you both for lunch Harry?"

"Yes, of course Andrew. Why don't we meet at the Old Ship hotel in the Mess bar? You remember, where Winnie had lunch that day? Does that sound okay for you?"

"Sounds absolutely perfect. Maybe, if Eugene the waiter is on duty we could ask him about Winnie?"

"Yes, good idea but I will leave that in your capable hands. My wife doesn't like me questioning people when we are out together socially. Is 1.30pm okay with you? I will book a table."

"Absolutely fine thanks."

Harry and his wife Liz arrived at the Old Ship hotel just before 1.30. They had taken a taxi for the short journey to make a break from driving. Just as they were being shown to their table Andrew walked in.

"Over here Andrew, brilliant timing." He ambled over to them. "Let me introduce you to my wife Liz."

"Pleased to meet you. May I call you Liz?"

"Of course Andrew and lovely to meet you too. How are you settling in here? Harry tells me your home is in Newcastle, that's a long way from Brighton."

"I'm cool thanks Liz. I love it here it's such a cosmopolitan city. I phone my parents every week to keep in touch and that saves them worrying about me. I must say Harry is exceptional and I am learning so much from him."

"As long as it's all the right things Andrew?"

"Right," Harry intervened, maybe before Andrew mentioned special keys, "let's order lunch. I'm hungry. Are we all okay with the Sunday roast? I'm told it's very good here."

"Fine with me Harry."

"Now, drinks. Liz and I like a bottle of Grand vin de Bordeaux with a roast. What about you Andrew?"

"A diet Coke for me please Harry."

Harry beckoned the waiter and placed their order.

The roast was exceptional or 'ab-so-lutely deee-lish!' in Andrew's words. It was a lovely change for him sat round a table with good company. Of late he had made do with takeaways on the sofa while watching tv.

"How about the New York cheesecake followed by a caffe Americano?" suggested Harry.

"Oh music to my ears!" beamed Andrew and Liz nodded appreciatively.

"We are going for a walk along the promenade to the Meeting Place before we get an Uber taxi back. What are you doing Andrew?"

"I'm going to see if Eugene is around. I would like to ask him a few questions regarding the case."

"Okay, just keep it basic and don't volunteer any information on Winnie."

"No. I won't. He probably already knows her funeral is on Tuesday as it's on the Brighton Radio streaming app."

"If you encounter any problems call me."

"Yes Harry, I will," and they all said their goodbyes.

"He seems a good lad Harry so make sure you look after him!" Liz advised her husband. "I like his dress code too - white Vans, white tee shirt and blue slacks - very snazzy - not like the way you dress Harry!"

Liz looked her husband up and down. He too was very smart but in a more traditional way, even boring. Yes, very boring compared to young Andrew!

He preferred a worsted wool suit for its comfort and non-creased look. On the upside this made it very durable; on the downside he seemed to have lived in it for years. Not exactly sexy! It bore a very discreet pattern of silver outlined squares on a bluish grey background he kept explaining to her proudly - which yes, if she squinted hard she could just about distinguish - but no, not sexy or snazzy.

"Perhaps you could try wearing something a little more 'with it' Harry?" She looked over towards her husband who was wearing a wry smile and purposely avoiding her gaze.

"Or perhaps pigs might fly eh Harry?" They both looked skywards and chuckled.

As they carried on walking along the promenade Liz noticed strips of blue police tape still hanging on the railings.

"Is that where the shooting took place Harry?"

"Yes, those strips should have been removed by now though. I will make sure the council is informed tomorrow."

Walking past the deckchair area Harry noticed Tom talking to another man, presumably his father.

"Just hang on a minute Liz, I would like a word with Tom the deckchair attendant."

"Okay. I'll take a look round the shops."

"Tom. How are you? Is this your father?"

"Yes Sir."

Harry explained to Tom's dad how he was the investigating detective for the murder in one of his son's deckchairs and how terrible it must have been for Tom at the time.

"Are you going to the funeral next Tuesday Tom?"

"Yes Sir. It was mentioned on the Brighton news stream this morning. My dad is going to look after the deckchairs for me and mum is going to drive me to Littlehampton."

Chapter 5

Eureka!

"That's good Tom. I will see you there. Take care and bye for now."

Harry ran to catch up with Liz. "How much have you spent then?"

"Nothing today Harry. I didn't have my credit card on me."

"Phew! Thank goodness!" he laughed. "That's saved us applying for a second mortgage," he added with a feigned sigh of relief.

They arrived at the Meeting Place cafe. Outside a group of people had gathered watching a smaller group playing with heavy metal balls. Liz was curious so Harry explained it was the local Pétanque Club playing boules. It was the fastest growing sport in the UK.

"Maybe you could play when you retire Harry?"

"I might ... either that or golf or maybe lawn bowls at Worthing but I have at least another two years work ahead of me first. Come on, let's cross the road and get an Uber taxi. I'm ready for a cup of tea then I'll finish the crossword."

"Yes, and after that fall asleep no doubt! I don't know, eat, sleep, worsted wool crease resistant suits ... mind you don't get too excited Harry!" She sighed sarcastically at her otherwise lovely husband.

"Eh? Oh no. I won't."

"Harry finished his cuppa along with a slice of Liz's homemade lemon drizzle cake and carried on where he left off on the Sunday crossword. Suddenly he dropped his pen and threw his arms triumphantly in the air as he shouted, "E U R E K A ! Got it!" as loud as his voice could shout.

"Got what Harry?"

"Oh, it's a strange one Liz but we found some Greek numbers engraved on the back of a Rolex watch."

"So ..." questioned Liz even more puzzled.

"So ... one of the answers to a clue I have here is 'bank safe deposit box'."

"S O ?" Asked Liz even louder. "Explain Harry!"

"So Liz, my love, I'm certain that's what the numbers represent on the watch - the code for a safe deposit box in a Cyprus bank!"

"Ahhh! I'm sure that makes sense to you Harry, so I'm pleased for you."

"It's highly likely we will be going to Cyprus next week to continue our investigations."

"Well ensure you look after young Andrew and make sure he phones his parents."

"I will Liz. He is very keen to get involved and learns at the rate of knots. He sees me as his mentor and wants to emulate me one day."

Liz smiled at her husband. She was very proud of him but couldn't help but quip - "Just as long as he doesn't dress like you ..."

Harry smiled to himself. "We have to go to Winnie's funeral at Littlehampton on Tuesday, so it may be just after that."

All too soon the 8am Monday meeting was underway.

"Morning Harry, morning Andrew," greeted DCS Street. "I have asked Angela to join us as she will be making some bookings for you later. What did you find out from your phone calls to the police superintendent at Palmers Green station and from Yiannis Galanis the police chief in Nicosia Angela?"

… Andrew ran his fingers protectively and with immense relief through his hair … then sent a silent memo to himself: Mouth to brain - never, ever make a bet with Harry Webb!

"From my call to Palmers Green I established Andreas Athanasiou's parents came to England in 1974 after the Turkish military invasion. Their home was destroyed, in fact the whole village was bombed and to this day is still unoccupied. After about six weeks of them leaving Palmers Green, sharing a home with another family, Andreas was born. His parents, with the help of friends, opened a Greek Meze takeaway and they lived over the premises. It was very successful.

Andreas was good at school but as a teenager he became mixed up with a gang selling drugs. His father was very tough on him to put it mildly so he left home. He was subsequently arrested several times and is well known by the Palmers Green police. He always managed to escape going to jail though. The superintendent said they had lost touch with him but suspect he may be involved with an East End gang.

I managed to speak to Mr Yiannis Galanis in Nicosia, though it was a little difficult with the time difference. I gave him the name of the other man, Andreas Athanasiou. He said he would make some enquiries though thought it may prove difficult. He will phone you later today Sir."

"Thank you Angela. Now, I have another job for you today. Would you please book Harry and Andrew on an Easy Jet flight to Larnaca, Cyprus on Wednesday at 12.15pm. You will need their passport details." Angela nodded.

The DCS shuffled through a few papers on his desk, "And the next booking Angela is at the Holiday Inn, in Nicosia. Best not to confirm the number of nights. When you have made the bookings I will phone Yiannis Galanis and he no doubt will arrange for someone to meet them both at the airport and take them to their hotel.

First though would you please ring the R.S. hospital and ask if Mr Grey is still there or if he has been discharged. If he is home Harry and Andrew please go to see how he is."

John Street leaned back in his chair, with a big sigh, "Right Harry where are we with this case?"

"Well Sir, I hope Cyprus has the answers to these pertinent questions:

Why was Mr Pantazis shot dead on our beach?

Why was Winnie Williams beaten up in her home?

Was it only the euros the thugs were after?

Did they know about the diamonds?

Why did Winnie have Mr Pantazis's phone number?

Why was My Grey shot?

Why were the diamonds hidden behind the car radios?

Where are the two men who worked in the unit at Gatwick?

Why were these two men carrying guns?

Why have they scarpered to Cyprus?

Where do they live/hole out in Cyprus?

Why did Mr Castellanos delay his flight to Gatwick?

Who tells who which car to hire from Mr Grey's garage? Is he involved?

Could he be being blackmailed?

Who hired the unit at Gatwick?

Who is the man who dined with Mr Pantazis in The Grand and visited the surround sound unit at Gatwick?

Who is the lady in the photograph and where is she now? England or Cyprus?

All the above questions need answers." Harry sat forward in his seat. "When we go to Winnie's funeral tomorrow I want to have a word with Clive Bowman, Winnie's brother in law. He apparently works at Haywards Heath. I would like to know where exactly."

Angela knocked and entered. "Excuse me Sir. I have just heard back from the hospital. Mr Grey was sent home on Friday evening. I have his address here for Andrew's sat-nav. The flights are booked for Wednesday as requested. Should I ask Bob to take Harry and Andrew to Gatwick?"

"Yes please Angela and ask him to make sure he gets them there in good time!"

"Harry and Andrew, you can go now to Haywards Heath to have a word with Mr Grey."

"Fine Sir."

On the way Harry asked Andrew to call into the Classic garage first for a chat with Stan and Alex. While they were there they could kill two birds with one stone by checking the back door had been repaired.

Andrew pulled up at the front but there appeared to be no one about so they went round the back, there both mechanics were working on one of the black MGBs.

Alex called out, "Hi can I help you? Oh, you are the two police detectives."

"Yes, we are just on our way to see Max and thought we would call in for a few words. I see the broken door has been repaired."

"Yes Sir, Mrs Grey arranged it through the insurance company."

"Are you still working full time on the cars and taking some over to the 6 speaker unit at Gatwick?"

"Mrs Grey asked us to keep the cars in good order but not to take any more over to Gatwick. She heard it had been shut down anyway."

"Do you have any cars out on hire at the moment?"

"Mrs Grey said her and her husband would deal with any hire cars."

"What do you know about Mr Grey being shot here? Any further details?"

"No, very little Sir. Mrs Grey called in on her way to visit him at the Royal Sussex and told us he would probably be home by Friday night."

"Okay, thanks for your help. We will let you get on with your work now. We're off to have a word with the Grey's."

As they left Andrew asked Harry of his thoughts on Stan and Alex and did he think they were genuine.

"I do Andrew. If they were connected in any way to the diamonds they would have scarpered by now like the two thugs at the Gatwick unit."

Andrew's sat-nav took them straight to the Grey's house.

"Well, lovely residence isn't it Andrew? This must have cost a pretty penny! Let's ring and see if Mr Grey is at home."

Mrs Grey answered the door. "Yes," she asked.

"They both held out their ID cards and Harry told her they would very much like a word with her husband. If he was up to it of course.

"Yes, but please keep it short. Max is still recovering from the shock of being shot. He was so lucky the bullet only clipped his shoulder you know."

Harry and Andrew followed her through to the lounge where Mr Grey was outstretched on the sofa. His shoulder was heavily strapped and he looked pretty rough.

"Thanks for seeing us Mr Grey. I promise we won't stay long but could we please ask you a few questions pertinent to our immediate enquiries?"

"You've got a captive audience boys!" he jested. "But was I an idiot? A real idiot! That black Ford you told me to look out for was parked directly outside the garage window - and what did I do? I know, I know, I should have done what you asked and rung you straight away but stupidly I marched straight in didn't I? Prize clodhopper!"

"What happened next Mr Grey?"

"As soon as they clapped eyes on me they both pulled out guns and wanted to know what I had done with their diamonds. Their diamonds? I told them I didn't have a clue what they were talking about. Not a Scooby! One of them went absolutely berserk and screamed he would shoot me if

I didn't tell them. I have omitted his disgusting expletives for the sake of your ears gentlemen."

Mr Grey swallowed and caught his breath. "I ran! They ran after me!"

He closed his eyes, swallowing once again.

"I swiftly ducked. Bang! They shot me in the shoulder. Instinctively, survival instinct like, I played dead. It seemed the obvious thing to do."

He paused taking another long breath. "It convinced them though, didn't it? One of them shouted, 'He's dead, let's get out of here'. The acting emanated from my love of cowboy films. I used to love doing the death roll and holding my breath when I was a young lad. I hoped they'll hop it if they thought they had killed me!"

He gave a nervous little laugh before closing his eyes.

"Just a couple more questions Mr Grey I can see you are tired. Could you tell from their accents if they were English?"

"No, no, definitely not! I would say they were Greek as they sounded just like that Mr Pantazis."

"And the last one for now, you said you were asked about diamonds. Presumably you don't know about any diamonds or you would have said while being held at gunpoint?"

"Well, exactly! Exactly! I have no idea of any diamonds no idea at all. Also I must say I am really sorry I was so short with you both and your DCS Street from the onset. I was really stressed over crippling financial matters."

"Well Mr and Mrs Grey, hold on to your hats, I'm afraid you have unwittingly been dragged into a very serious crime involving diamond smuggling."

"What! How? W..h..a..t ?"

We have discovered two of your MGB cars, the red one and the white one had small bags of diamonds hidden behind their radios."

"No! Really? Really? So that's why I had to take them to that unit at Gatwick! He was very insistent I used them to install the 6 speaker radios."

"Who was Mr Grey?"

"Bert Barber. His card is pinned on the notice board in the office at the garage. He has a company in Dulwich in London's East End.

"Could you describe him please?" asked Andrew.

"Yes. He is quite smartly dressed a bit like a London spiv, yes just like a London spiv he is, a wide boy if ever I saw one! Bit Greek in appearance though so I should say a Greek spiv! Is there such a thing? Dunno, but that describes him to a T. A right weird one. He has a very noticeable white streak through his thick black hair."

Harry and Andrew looked at each other.

"Mr Barber eh? Strange as you say a Greek man having such an English sounding name! Yes, we know of a man fitting that description Mr Grey. Thank you so much for your help and we sincerely hope you make a full recovery soon. Could we call in at your garage on the way back to the station to look at Mr Barber's card?"

"Yes of course. My wife will pre warn Stan. Let me know if I can be of any further help."

"What do you think of Max Grey now Harry?" asked Andrew as they pulled away.

"Well, when we first met him I thought he was involved for sure with the diamonds but not now. He genuinely looked shocked when we told him about them a minute ago. Besides, I bet he would have kept them for himself if he knew they were in his cars! That man is in serious financial difficulties.

... I'm not quite so sure about her though ..." he added.

"Andrew, do you remember when we interviewed Gino the head waiter at The Grand?" Andrew nodded. "Well, he described in detail the lady Mr Dimitris Pantazis was dining with didn't he? He also confirmed she was the same lady on the photograph we found in the safe. Then he described the man with the white streak in his hair."

"Yes, I remember Harry, but what's your concern?"

"We never went back to get photos from the CCTV footage did we?"

"Oh no! We were so engrossed with the contents of the safe ... when we get back to the station I will go over and collect them. We ought to have them on our phones."

"Thanks Andrew. I so want to know about this guy with the white streak. Is he indeed Mr Bert Barber? Oh, we're at the garage already - how time flies when you're thinking! Let's have a look in Max Grey's office."

Stan and Alex watched as the car pulled up at the rear of the building.

"Hello again you two. How was Max Grey?"

"He's all strapped up but recovering slowly. It could be a while before he is back here though. I expect he will be on the phone to you soon. We would like to have a quick look in his office please."

"It's locked at the moment but I will just fetch the key," offered Stan.

As he walked off Andrew winked at Harry and whispered, "Saves you using your keys!"

Stan unlocked the office door. "Is there anything particular you want to see Sir?"

"Yes Stan, just a business card pinned on your notice board. Ah, here it is ... Mr Bert Barber, Managing Director, 6 Speaker Surround Sound Systems - quite an alliterative tongue twister that, don't you think?

I'm certain that's a London phone number and ah good! There's an email address here too. Take a photo Andrew. Now, let's have a look on the back ... a Cyprus phone number eh ... photograph that too!"

Andrew obliged.

"Thanks Stan, you can lock up now. Tell me, did you ever see this man Bert Barber?"

"Yes, he called in a few times to speak to Mr Grey. He also arranged for us to take certain cars to Gatwick to be fitted with the surround sound systems. That's all I know Sir. He sounded and looked Greek. 'Bert Barber' doesn't really suit him."

"Thanks Stan that is very useful. We have to return at some point though."

On the way to the station Andrew tried ringing the London number on loud speaker. Back came the reply, 'This number is no longer available'.

"Try the Cyprus number Andrew."

That number did ring and requested the caller to leave a short message.

"Don't say a word Andrew, just hang up."

"Okay. I could try the email though?"

"Yes, just send an enquiry regarding their 6 speaker systems."

Andrew did try but it was later returned 'not recognisable'.

"So Harry, just where is Mr Bert Barber do you think? This man is proving to be quite an enigma."

Back at the station Harry confirmed the day's meetings both at the garage and Mr Grey's home. Angela said she would update the DCS then on looking around asked, "Where's Andrew then?"

"Oh, he's down at The Grand hotel, just picking something up for me."

"Is your bag packed for Cyprus Harry?"

"No, I don't think so, not yet. I leave all that to Liz."

"Well you make sure you look after young Andrew while you're away! It's fine for you, you know the country well but this is completely new territory for him."

Andrew turned up about forty minutes later. "How did you get on?" asked Harry.

"Fine thanks. The maintenance man was very helpful and I have some good photographs. I will put them on yours and Angela's screen shots. He did want to know why I needed them so I told him it was for an ongoing investigation."

"Well done Andrew! We might as well knock off now. See you here in the morning before we go to Winnie's funeral."

Next morning at Littlehampton Crematorium Harry and Andrew took seats at the rear. Linda, Winnie's sister and her husband Clive were in the front row along with Mary Mills and another man, presumably Colin from number 2. A few others joined the little throng who Harry did not know. Tom the deckchair attendant sat nearer the back along with another man ...

"That's Eugene the waiter from the Old Ship hotel," whispered Andrew. "I had a few words with him on Sunday after you left. He explained Winnie was a regular customer, at least two or three days a week, though sometimes many more, so he was very upset to hear of her death.

I asked if he was aware of her activities and although she never told him he did guess. He saw her go into the ladies after her lunch and come out a different woman!

He was somewhat comforted though by the fact she enjoyed a delicious meal with wine on her last day."

Harry nodded.

Chapter 6

Kleftiko or Stifado?

The celebrant was just closing proceedings after portraying wonderfully the beautiful but sadly foreshortened life of dear Winnie by the nefarious actions of beings unknown.

Then to the haunting, dulcet chords of 'You'll Never Walk Alone' the curtains were drawn on Winnie Williams.

The small gathering went outside to admire her floral tributes. Harry and Andrew had a few words with Mary, who introduced Colin from number 2. They were both visibly distraught.

"How is your leg Mary?" asked Andrew.

"It's so much better thanks to you two. I have a community nurse in every morning now ... Doesn't Gerry Marsden sing that song so lovely? Carousel was Winnie's favourite musical you know and she would watch a Liverpool footie match just to hear the crowd sing along to their anthem. I told the celebrant that."

Andrew smiled. "We are so pleased you are getting help Mary but you take care."

Harry asked Andrew to have a few words with Winnie's sister as he wanted a quiet word with her husband Clive.

Harry introduced himself to Clive and showed his ID card. First he asked how Linda was coping and if everything was being sorted out in Winnie's apartment. Clive was a little hesitant in replying. He explained they were still waiting for probate to be sorted before they could clear the property yet alone put it on the market.

"Sure, I understand that can indeed take a while and usually does unfortunately. I know this may not be a good time but could I ask you please where you are employed?"

"Yes Sir, I have no problem with that. I have been employed for the last five years at a car parts company, Auto Spares of East Grinstead. It's north of Haywards Heath off the A22."

"And just one more question, do you deliver car parts to the Classic Car Company not far from Haywards Heath?"

"Yes Sir. I know it well. They buy spark plugs, filters and both side and headlight bulbs for their older cars from us. I know Mr Grey the owner. He has some really valuable cars in his showroom you know. On the news it reported he had been shot by burglars. How is he now?"

"He is recovering at home but it will be a while before he's back at the garage.

Thank you Clive, we may require you to answer a few more questions at a later date though. In the meantime if you could please give your mobile number and email to my assistant detective Andrew Brown here that will be fine for now."

Linda caught Harry's attention and thanked him for coming along. She was very tearful which made it difficult for Harry to ask her any questions so all he could say was how sorry he was for Winnie's untimely death.

"Have they found out who did it yet?" she sobbed.

"No, not yet I'm afraid but please believe me we are absolutely committed to solving this whole nasty business as soon as we can. Clive told me you were still waiting on probate?"

"Yes Sir. I do hope it will not be much longer then we can put her apartment on the market."

"Well, if I can help in any way please give me a call. You have my number."

"Yes Sir, and thank you."

Harry walked over to Mary. "I just wanted to say how sorry I was you had to find Winnie that way Mary. It must have been dreadful for you. Would you know if she had many visitors at all?"

"Well, not usually but recently a man came by in the evening. Colin told me he had a very flashy car. He could tell you the make but all cars look the same to me."

"Did you get a good look at him at all?"

"Well, I'm not that great on remembering faces especially without my specs but I can tell you he was smartly dressed with a distinctive white streak in his hair. I was curious so did ask Winnie about him but she clammed up and flatly refused to tell me anything about him. I thought that very strange. We were friends you know ..."

"Thanks Mary, that's very interesting. Maybe I could have a word with Colin?"

Harry asked Andrew to grab a few quick words with Eugene, mainly to establish his nationality.

Colin came over and introduced himself to Harry.

"Hello Colin. Mary tells me a flashy car parked by your end of the block lately. Can you tell me what make it was please?"

"Yes Sir. It was a silver blue Audi. I only ever saw the back of the man who drove it but Mary said he went to Winnie's apartment."

"Thank you Colin. If you recall anything else could you please call the police station and leave a message for me?" Harry passed him a card.

Andrew then came over, they both said their farewells and left. Andrew said his chat with Eugene had proved fruitful. He was apparently half Romanian and half Turkish.

"I asked if he was a Turkish Cypriot as I remembered what you had told me about the Turkish invasion. He said he was but then kept shtum."

"Good work Andrew! We will ask Angela if she can find out more about him while we're away."

Harry told Andrew about the silver blue Audi and the re-emergence of the man with the silver streak in his hair. Bert Barber? No! Alias? More than likely!

"I'll tell you what Andrew I've heard of paths crossing but we are dealing with ruddy Spaghetti Junction on steroids here!" Harry muttered.

"Everyone we've interviewed seems to be interconnected with someone else: Winnie had Mr Pantazis's number and received a visit from the man with the white streak in his hair. Clive Bowman knows Max Grey - he supplied parts to him. The printers at Gatwick worked next door to two or three suspects and knew of the man with the white streak! Who of these are innocent by standers and who are linked to a murder and diamond smuggling?"

It was late afternoon when they returned to the station. "It sounds as though you picked up a lot of information today chaps?" chirped Angela. "Just read your reports."

"We did Angela and as we are off to Cyprus tomorrow could you please follow up a few of these leads for us? Most Importantly do checks on Eugene from the Old Ship and on Clive Bowman, Linda's husband. Text us with anything of interest."

Angela laughed sarcastically, "That's great! You two swan off to sunny Cyprus and expect me to do the donkey work for you here!"

"But Angela, didn't you always say you wanted to be a detective? Well, here's your chance!"

"Oh, go on you two, I will do what I can. Go get your bags packed and have a good flight. Text me when you arrive in Cyprus."

"Yes Angela," they chanted in unison as they left.

"See you tomorrow Andrew."

"Yes Harry. Bob has confirmed he will pick me up from here. We will then drive on to your place for 10.15am."

"Great. That will be in good time for the 12.15 to Larnaca. Remember your passport Andrew. I have exchanged some Stirling for euros to give us a small wad of spending money. It's a four and a half hour flight - time for you to read up more on Cyprus! Learn a few key words you think might prove useful. Local time will be 17.45 when we land.

The police in Cyprus have arranged to meet us at the airport then take us on to the Holiday Inn in Metaxas Square, Nicosia. We should check in around 18.45. It's a great hotel. I stayed eight years ago when my brother was in an American hospital there.

I'm getting a bit ahead of myself here Andrew but after we check in tomorrow just dump your holdall in your room. I would like to take you straight to my favourite Greek restaurant. I particularly like the Stifado beef or Kleftiko lamb with a Keo beer, then a baklava for sweet followed by a brandy sour made with the silky smooth local Metaxa brandy ..."

"Sounds good Harry but you are making me feel so hungry and we are not even leaving until tomorrow!" Andrew interrupted.

"Sorry I won't mention it again until we get there ... apart from mine will probably be the Kleftiko lamb - traditionally cooked for hours in underground ovens, so deliciously tender ..."

Harry stopped midstream. He could feel Andrew's piercing eyes on him and as he turned slowly to meet his gaze he pulled out the folded white handkerchief from his top pocket and waved it as a peace gesture. They both laughed.

The following morning Bob picked up Andrew at the police station and they drove on to pick up Harry. Liz waved them off from the front door with instructions to take care and stay out of trouble.

"Why are you going to Gatwick then?" asked Bob.

"Continuing our investigations in Cyprus Bob, but we can't really elaborate, sorry."

"No probs 'arry, I won't say a word," he promised tapping the side of his nose with his index finger. "Ere we are. Have a good trip and I'll see you when you get back."

"Cheers Bob."

Once in the lounge Harry bought his usual Americano and Andrew his Coke. They both relaxed reading newspapers.

"What do you think we should expect to find in Cyprus Harry?"

"Well, one thing is certain, it is not going to be easy! When we meet up with Mr Yiannis Galanis in the morning I am hoping he will be able to take us to where Dimitris Pantazis lived. We need him to pass on all the local information he has. We also need to know what he has found out about Nico Castellanos and the other two who got the flight out - Andreas Athanasiou and Yirgos Papadopoulos.

We will have to be careful how we handle things with this police force Andrew and should Yirgos Papadopoulos go over to the Turkish side matters will become very complicated. We would need to deal with the Turkish police then too, not easy! Things will become clearer tomorrow though hopefully."

As the plane took off Andrew was as excited as a young lad going to his first FA Cup final.

"Could we swap seats Harry? I would like to get a few photos of the Pyrenees. I'm keen on taking a holiday in the south of France sometime to have a go at climbing the mountain range."

"No problem Andrew. Did you manage to read up on Cyprus and learn a few key words?"

"Well, I made a start. I found it a very interesting island so it was relatively easy to take in a few facts and I learnt a handful of words too ... yassou, hello; kalimera, good morning; kalispera, good night and yamas, cheers. I hope we have time to use the latter!"

"Well that's a good start Andrew. You will learn a lot more while we are working there, but no swear words mind! So what did you learn on the history of the island?"

"I have concentrated mainly on the EOKA Greek conflict in the late 1950s where tragically 412 servicemen were killed and the green line is still, would you believe, manned today by the United Nations. I also touched on the Turkish military invasion in 1974 where some of the villages caught up in the conflict are still lying unoccupied. Can you even comprehend that Harry?"

"Yes, that's correct Andrew and so interesting you touched on that as I'm worried it could throw a few problems our way this week."

"How?"

"Well, we could well have to work with the Turkish police and the United Nations. When we get back I will lend you one of my books on Cyprus. They are very detailed and informative.

Can we send emails while we are flying Andrew?"

"Yes, I should think so by now, but I will just check with the steward."

Andrew asked a very attractive stewardess who passed by, "Yes, we don't have any problems now Sir," she smiled.

"Why did you ask Harry?"

"My mind has been constantly churning over and over regarding Eugene from the Old Ship. I did ask Angela to question the management on basics like how long he had been employed there but I want her to delve deeper. For example does he holiday to Cyprus or to Turkey and are there any other gems she can wheedle out of them that could be pertinent."

"No probs, I will send it now."

At that moment the hostess trundled a trolley along the aisle.

"I'm having the ham and cheese toasted sandwich with a coffee please," Harry smiled at her ... "and you Andrew?"

"Yes, I'll have the toasted sandwich too but with a Coke thanks."

As they sipped their drinks the plane smoothly passed over the Pyrenees.

"Andrew could you tell me about your background? Your parents, schooling, how you decided on your career etc?"

"Certainly. My mother is a nurse, a sister in fact and my father a general builder. I have a younger sister at University College in Edinburgh. I was fortunate enough to have an excellent schooling, achieving top marks in many subjects:

I passed 12 examinations with top grades in GCSE, they are what you would have referred to as 'O' levels I then went on to take 4 'A' levels. I achieved a 9 in both English and Maths - which equates to A** to your generation and an 8 and 7 in Physical Education and Physics respectively - an A* and A.

My tutors wanted me to go on to University but my brain felt addled after years of studying to the extent I couldn't face any more learning so I got a job advertised in a call centre. Initially it was a luxurious holiday for the old grey matter! The work was okay and I secured many commissions. I liked the others working there, they were a cheerful bunch but some of the customer abuse was demoralising so I left after a year. I worked as part of a maintenance crew then for a while.

Not too keen on that I read in the newspaper the police were recruiting so I applied and was accepted. Thankfully I passed the entry exams and was soon walking the beat in Newcastle. After nine months I was called to the superintendent's office and he asked if I'd like to further my career by going to the Police Training College at Hendon for seventeen weeks. If successful there I would be posted to the London Metropolitan Police.

I jumped at the chance as it was a tremendous opportunity. I completed the course with top marks, including the driving and the shooting. It felt great engaging my brain once again. After six months I was asked if I would like to move to a police apartment in Brighton, working with the crime department. So here I am Harry, with you!"

"Is there anything about the job you don't like?"

He contemplated before answering. "Well, there was something yesterday Harry that made me feel ... well, I suppose uncomfortable is the word."

"What was that?"

"At Winnie's funeral you asked me to talk to Mary but she, along with the others, were so consumed with grief I felt we were intruding on their privacy."

"And you gave her a wonderful warm smile Andrew, I saw you and believe me your compassion on the day was commendable. We had to be there. We gathered so much information by so many in such a short time which will go on to solving these horrific murders quicker. Now, is anything else playing on your mind?"

Andrew looked quizzically over to Harry, "One thing I wondered - how come it's us flying out to Cyprus on this case, why not other police?"

"I'll come to that in a moment Andrew, but first I must tell you I was very pleased with your detailed replies. DCS Street phoned me last evening, giving me your background but I needed to hear it from you."

"Blimey! You were checking up on me?"

"Yes Andrew as it's vital to my position. I will explain. The DCS said I should tell you but you must keep this confidential as no one apart from the DCS knows I am not just Harry Webb DCI. I am in fact an undercover detective working for the Special Branch."

Andrew sat transfixed with a gaping jaw ...

"How you see me now, a staid, middle aged family man is not always as I am. I was asked to come to Brighton as we had a tip off a shooting was about to occur."

Andrew physically pushed his dropped jaw back into place. "Crikey Harry, I was not expecting that!"

Harry laughed. "Oh my word you would not recognise me with long, unkempt hair and tattoos all over my face and neck! Your deliciously fragrant hairdresser would blow a gasket Andrew.

So why you, you ask? I need you to cover my back at all times. There are some evil and very dangerous men out there who would like nothing more than to put a bullet through me. I hope that explains 'why **us**'?"

Andrew, still processing what he had just heard replied, "Sure Harry, you'll have my support at all time."

It was a smooth flight and within the hour, as cabin crew were making their final checks, they started their descent. Over the tannoy the pilot announced landing at Larnaca airport would be in ten minutes and thanked them for flying with Easy Jet.

After landing they soon cleared customs and as they went through to arrivals they spotted two Cypriot police officers. They looked smart in their blue short sleeved shirts, navy trousers, light blue jackets and blue berets. They wore guns in waist holsters.

"Crikey, I wouldn't argue with them!" exclaimed Andrew.

The two officers spotted Harry and Andrew and ambled over to them introducing themselves and welcoming them.

"Yiassoo perakalo, Mr Harry Webb and Mr Andrew Brown. I will continue to speak to you in English."

"Thank you," replied Andrew.

"We are under instruction to take you to the Holiday Inn in Metaxas Square, Nicosia and to pick you up at 9am tomorrow when we will take you on to our Police Headquarters at Platy Aglantzia, Lefkosia for a meeting with the chief of the Nicosia police, Mr Yiannis Galanis."

"Efharisto," Harry thanked them.

"Oh, you speak some Greek Mr Harry?"

"Yes, just a little."

"Fine, and maybe you will learn more while you are here Mr Andrew?"

They arrived at the Holiday Inn in just under an hour in the speedily driven police car.

"Antio sas. Goodbye, we will see you here tomorrow at 9am."

Harry and Andrew collected their holdalls from the boot of the police car and entered Peoewiov, Reception.

"Kalispera," Harry greeted the receptionist.

"Good evening to you too," replied the receptionist seemingly surprised at Harry's Greek. "We do speak good English Sir if you would prefer. Do you have a booking with us?"

"Yes," for Mr Harry Webb and Mr Andrew Brown."

"Thank you, yes. We have been expecting you. If you would please complete and sign the booking forms I will give you your keys. Could I have your passports please? We keep all passports in the safe."

After signing the forms Harry and Andrew were given their keys. They had been allocated rooms on the fourth floor, 412 and 426. Harry had a large front facing room with a good view over Metaxas Square, Andrew's, however was a much smaller back room.

While they were in the lift Harry reminded Andrew to leave the unpacking until later. He was anxious to get down to his favourite restaurant in Ledra Street. The sandwiches on the plane now seemed a lifetime away and his stomach was grumbling angrily.

"Okay Harry, I'm fine with that."

As they were walking down Ledra Street Andrew asked if this was the infamous 'murder mile' he had read about.

"Yes Andrew. It was very dangerous for the Army and Air Force men on patrol. Many of them and other security forces were killed down here. It's good to see it thriving now though as a popular tourist attraction with so many lovely restaurants and shops."

Andrew nodded in agreement.

"We're nearly there Andrew, just by the green line ... and Ahhh Yes! It's open! See, the Romanzo Taverna. Let's see if Zaikai is still the owner."

Harry and Andrew were just entering the heaving restaurant when out of nowhere a very large man with a long beard, clad in a massive apron ran over to Harry, flinging his arms round him in one ginormous bear hug.

"Kalispera o filos mou Harry," he boomed.

"And good evening to you Zaikai. Meet my friend Andrew. Can we converse in English now please?"

"Yes of course and good evening to you too Andrew. It's so good to see you again Harry. Please take this seat by the window gentlemen and I will fetch you our special menu."

"Thank you Zaikai, if it hasn't changed though I will probably know exactly what's on it."

Zaikai laughed heartily, "Yes, it's still the same and from what I remember you used to alternate between the beef and the lamb?"

"Oh! What a memory. That's right. So do you have the beef Stifado tonight?"

"But of course Harry and it's the best! Would you both like that served with green beans and potatoes?"

They both nodded appreciatively and Harry ordered a Keo and a Coke.

After the main course, which Andrew thought was even more delicious than Harry had described, Harry opted for baklava and Andrew the ice cream. Just as they were finishing Zaikai came over insisting they have a drink on the house. Harry opted for a brandy sour and Andrew another Coke.

Zaikai brought three drinks over and drawing up a chair joined them in a medley of nostalgic, jolly and idle chitchat. The evening flew by. As the restaurant emptied Zaikai offered to give them a lift back to the hotel after he had cleared the tables and locked up.

Andrew gasped in sheer delight when Zaikai appeared from behind the restaurant driving a bright yellow Aston Martin with gleaming accessories.

"What?" he gasped, "oh what!"

"Jump in and I will give you a ride round by the green line and back to Metaxas Square."

Andrew remained speechless for a while, just the odd, 'what?' escaping from his voice box. "I want one just like it!" he eventually managed to say. "What an absolute whiz!

I wonder if it is fitted with a 6 speaker surround sound system," he jested with Harry.

All too soon they pulled up to the Holiday Inn.

"Antio sas. Ta leme."

"Good night to you too Zaikai and yes, we will definitely see you again before we fly home," replied Harry.

"Just too right," agreed Andrew, longingly watching the Aston Martin disappearing from sight.

As they entered reception Andrew said he was going to ask for a room change as his was quite a tiny single and he suffered badly from claustrophobia.

"I don't think you will get it changed now Andrew as they only have a night porter on duty. Look, you take my room for now and we can sort it out in the morning. I can sleep on a clothes line!"

"Thanks Harry, I really appreciate that. I will get my holdall."

They exchanged keys, said their good nights and agreed to meet for breakfast in the dining room at 8am.

Next morning Harry was up before 7 o'clock so decided to take a walk around the old part of Nicosia. He was back in the dining room for 8 o'clock, informing the waiter he would require a table for two. He ordered bacon, scrambled eggs and toast with coffee.

Andrew was usually punctual but there was no sign of him yet. Harry tried ringing his mobile and his room but there was no answer on either phone.

He finished his breakfast then tried ringing again. Still no answer on either phone so rather concerned he asked the head waiter to contact the chambermaid on the fourth floor and ask her to check on room 412.

The head waiter soon reported back. "The chambermaid has actually been working in the room opposite Sir. She heard two phones ringing but when she knocked on room 412 no one answered."

"Okay, thanks. I had better go up and see if he is alright."

"May I suggest you ask Alex the day security officer to go with you? He is just sat having a coffee over there." The waiter gesticulated to his right. "If you explain the circumstances he will be able to let you in as they are hot on security here."

Harry went over for a word with Alex explaining the situation. They checked with reception then both went up in the lift.

Alex rapped on the door of room 412 then opened it. Harry was horrified at the scene that met his eyes ...

... Andrew's clothes were strewn over the floor and his empty holdall was lying upside down on the bed.

"He's been abducted." Harry muttered. He knew Andrew would not have given in without a fight, he was not of that ilk.

"The maid said she heard two phones ring so I will just try Andrew's mobile once again ..."

A loud ringing emitted from under the bed. Harry fell down onto his hands and knees where he clocked both Andrew's wallet and mobile lying there side by side.

"So Alex, we need to establish quickly what exactly happened here and when. You have CCTV, yes?"

"Yes. Follow me Sir. I will lock this door and instruct the chambermaid not to enter. We can make our way down to the back entrance to check the CCTV. I will call the night duty security officer to ask if he heard or saw anything untoward."

"There will be two of your police here at 9am. Could you please request the reception desk to ask them to wait for me?"

"Yes of course Sir."

They soon reached the back entrance and Alex went into the 'Goods Receiving' office.

"Right. This is the CCTV camera ... let's have a look ... what time would you say?"

"I think it could have been soon after we returned last night," surmised Harry. "Try from 10.30 onwards."

Soon Alex squealed excitedly. "Look at this Sir, two masked men dressed in black and dragging along another man with a black sack over his head. It very much looks as though his hands are strapped behind his back. He is kicking out and resisting forcefully."

"Poor Andrew." exclaimed Harry, running his fingers anxiously through his thick black hair, while racking his brain for inspiration.

"Thank you Alex. The police will want a copy of this film. We had better report the whole sorry business to your management but ask if they could keep it under wraps until after our investigations."

"Yes Sir. I will report it now."

As they reached Reception the two police officers were waiting. Harry explained about Andrew being abducted and that a copy of the CCTV would be sent to them soon.

The Cypriot police were most concerned this had happened in their country. They suggested Harry get straight into the car and they drive him post haste to the office to meet up with Chief Yiannis Galanis as prearranged.

Mr Galanis met Harry at the entrance. His officers had phoned ahead and fully updated him.

"I'm horrified this should happen so soon after your arrival Harry," he reiterated.

Inside his office he instructed his two officers that none of the night's events should be disclosed to anyone, especially the press or any other media news outlets.

"We must organise a full search immediately. Please use your initiative in searching areas they could have feasibly taken Mr Brown to."

After the officers left Chief Galanis turned to Harry, "We had better inform your DCS John Street. Did he tell you I met him a few years ago while he was holidaying in Cyprus?"

"Yes Sir, he has fond memories of your country. He will not be at all happy to hear of last night's events though."

Mr Galanis's secretary put a call through to the Brighton police station and spoke with Angela initially who just managed to catch the DCS on his way out.

"Excuse me Sir but Chief Galanis is on the phone and wishes to speak to you urgently."

"Okay Angela, put him through. I do hope Harry and Andrew haven't found themselves in any trouble."

Yiannis Galanis explained all he knew about the abduction of Andrew Brown.

DCS Street turned white as he fell back in his chair. "WHAT !" he hollered. "How the hell could his happen? They have only been there a few hours for goodness sake!"

Angela came running into the office to see what the commotion was about so the DCS put the speakerphone on.

"Your DCI Harry Webb is with me now. I will pass him the phone."

"Harry. Tell me all you can. We must handle this with extreme care and under no circumstances allow this to make the foreign press or news media. Have you any idea who the perpetrators were?"

"I'm sure it's the same two men we have been after since the shooting of Mr Dimitris Pantazis on the beach Sir. It was probably me they wanted as they certainly didn't know Andrew and I had swapped rooms last night.

I had a look on the Holiday Inn CCTV footage. Andrew was putting up a brave fight but they managed to put a black sack over his head, tie his hands behind his back and bundle him out through the rear exit.

He did manage to kick his mobile phone and wallet under the bed though.The two men were certainly searching for something as they emptied his holdall leaving its contents strewn all over the floor.

Chief Galanis is putting out a search party covering the most probable places they could have taken him. I just hope he isn't in one of those remote villages taken over by the Turks after the military invasion.

If anyone can escape though Andrew can and his military training will be an invaluable asset in a crisis situation like this. You will put a freeze on any press release in the UK Sir?"

"Yes Harry, I will certainly do that. It goes without saying. Please inform me of any developments immediately they unfold."

"Of course Sir."

Harry solemnly handed the receiver back to Chief Galanis.

He asked Harry how he thought young Andrew would cope with the whole terrible situation.

"I am sure, even the slightest of opportunities he will turn to his advantage Sir. He is very alert. He is also extremely fit and an endurance runner as well being highly intelligent so let's just hope for that window of opportunity to open up for him very soon."

"I am utterly mystified as to why they took him ... They obviously did not know you two had changed rooms though and probably thought they were abducting you.

You were their target Harry. I will give you 24 hour protection with my best men while you are here."

Harry nodded.

"Now, let's have a look at the map and try to glean some inspiration as to where they might be holding him ...

They will obviously want him alive while it suits their plans otherwise they would have killed him in the hotel room. Have you any strong thoughts on this Harry? What is your gut telling you?"

"Well, unfortunately my gut is telling me a deserted old farmhouse first and foremost and probably close to the border. From what I can remember though there are a plethora of them scattered far and wide so where we begin will be absolute pot luck!

We must get started as soon as possible - if we don't find him by nightfall they could well cross the border - or worse still tire of keeping him alive!"

"I agree Harry, but first come with me to the armoury. We need to fit you out with a protective vest and gun. It's hot out there but it is essential for your protection."

It took no time to fit Harry out with the safety requisites - much less red tape involved it seemed than back in England. Before they could take so much as one step outside though Mr Galanis's secretary came bursting into the room, extremely emotional and flustered she cried out ...

"Biaouvn, hurry, hurry! Eneiyovtwg! Urgently please! It's the military police - oh my God, oh!" her eyes welled with tears - "they have found your Mr Andrew ..."

... Harry and Chief Yiannis Galanis froze in their tracks ... Harry's heart sank ...

116

Chapter 7

I'm propa paggered!

The night before, just after they returned from the sumptuous feast at Andreas's restaurant, Andrew let himself into his luxurious new room and flopped onto the bed. It had been an exhausting but memorable day for so many reasons and his mind was an eddy of Stifado beef; Harry being dressed as a longhaired undercover lout; Zaikai's Aston Martin - not to mention the mind blowing nature of his own important role with Harry and the unknown adventure to follow.

Inwardly smiling he heaved himself up and began to unpack essentials from his holdall. He couldn't get the Aston Martin out of his head. The entire situation was all a bit James Bondish he thought ... then, holding that thought ... he strode purposefully over to the full length mirror on the wall; focused forward; adopted the famous 007 stance; sleekly pulled his imaginary gun from its holster and with one well aimed shot killed the man walking menacingly towards him! He coolly blew the puff of smoke from the barrel and replaced the gun in it's holster.

"Gotcha!"

He hadn't played that out since he was a kid. He shook himself from his alter ego and became 'Andrew Brown' once more. The curtains were still open and the bright lights of Metaxas Square were well worth admiring for a few minutes more. His thoughts were then cruelly interrupted by a bang on his door.

"What's Harry forgotten?" He thought aloud as he opened the door, when -

THUMP! THUMP!! THUMP!!! He absorbed one to his head, one to his chest the other to his stomach. Utterly dazed he felt himself falling back onto the bed then being roughly shaken and punched over and over. A black cloth was then flung over his head ...

"Right, come on you, where is it? one yelled in a mixture of both Greek and English, while shaking him violently. "Tell me, tell me I say!"

"I don't know! I don't know what 'it' is!" He tried pulling himself up but was punched back down and one of the two men immediately strapped his hands behind his back. He kicked out and struggled desperately to free himself and to kick his mobile and wallet under the bed.

"Try retaliating again and we will kill you! Hear that? We will kill you!"

Not doubting their intentions for a moment he temporary went tight lipped and limp. The men then manhandled him out of the room, along the corridor to the service lift then out of the rear exit. Out in the open Andrew kicked and struggled to free himself for all his worth once more but he was bundled roughly into the back of a car which sped off into the night.

"We have you now Harry Webb!" one gloated. "We have you now at last!"

Realisation then struck Andrew - it was Harry they wanted but as they had swapped rooms the thugs had taken the wrong man. Initially he was so tempted to burst their bubble and put them straight by gloating himself, 'I'm not Harry Webb, you've taken the wrong man!' but decided against it. There would hopefully be a right time for that revelation. The car drove at breakneck speed, throwing him about like a rag doll in the back. Andrew estimated the journey had taken around an hour before the vehicle screeched to an abrupt halt. One of the men dragged him out so roughly the black cloth bag was dislodged from his head.

At this the other thug lost his cool and a torrent of abuse erupted from his mouth towards his partner. Andrew assumed they were swear words judging by the manner in which they were delivered.

"Too late now, just leave it off imbecile! He has already seen us and this farm you clumsy oaf so we will probably have to rejig our plans now ..."

It was about 2am and the full moon looked pitifully down on them. The farm was miserably dilapidated with numerous rat infested outbuildings and the inside of the house was not fit for human habitation. The roof leaked. It grew mould. It stank.

The angrier of the two men pushed him unceremoniously into a wonky, old fashioned, woodworm infested Windsor chair, strapping his arms to those of the chair's.

"We will be here all night. Sleep you!" grunted one, kicking him roughly across his legs.

The two thugs took no time at all before they were snoring - so shortly, Andrew planned, he would try to grab a few hours himself - but only after silently managing to loosen one of the rickety arms of the chair he was strapped in. He had swivelled himself to the side and whilst gripping the chair's right arm firmly pulled his own right arm back and forth, back and forth, back and forth many, many times.

He had been awake now for almost 24 hours and felt shattered, bruised and battered after the beating they had meted out to him. He closed his eyes.

In the morning his body clock told him it was around 7.30 when he first heard movement. He knew his only option was to escape. He had seen their faces after all and Mr Big would not be impressed with them.

One of the thugs announced he would go down to the village to pick up supplies. Andrew feigned being deep in sleep. The two men were still awaiting instructions on what to do with him next. They obviously still thought he was Harry Webb, and why shouldn't they?

As the angrier of the two left to fetch food Andrew 'awoke' and told the other one he needed the toilet. This hopefully would be his means of escape. His diafygi.

The man ignored him.

"If I don't get to the toilet pretty darn quick there will be one hell of a mess here for you to clear up!" Andrew shouted in earnest. "He'll make you do it won't he?"

"Okay. Be quick though, okay? Quick I say!" He bent over and undid his captive's ties.

Free, Andrew jumped up, gripped the wooden arm he had worked on and with one almighty wrench extricated it from the chair and smashed it relentlessly on the back of his captive's head. Thwack and thwack again!

The thug slumped to the floor unconscious.

Once outside Andrew immediately detected a track leading into a pine forest and ran and ran and ran for all he was worth. Neat adrenaline was now pumping through his veins and he did not stop for breath.

His combat training had taught him to run a zig zag course if ever caught in a situation like this - to make it impossible for anyone following, which he did to the letter, weaving a complex web between the tall pines.

Doggedly he continued his plight until eventually the trees thinned and the forest was a mere memory behind him. He was giddy with exhaustion.

So he allowed himself the luxury of briefly catching his breath and as he looked up noticed a series of large domes there in his eye-line, dominating the horizon.

At this point he breathed a huge sigh of relief and silently thanked Harry for being so insistent he should educate himself and read up on Cyprus during the flight. These domes ahead had unbelievably been the topic of his reading! Amazing. Only absolutely blooming amazing! He had known diddly squat about them before but now ...

"It's the RAF Radar Unit on Mount Olympus!" he puffed silently to himself.

Andrew picked up speed again and made a beeline to the unit's gate. By now the adrenaline rush was a mere whimper, he was weakening and the realisation of just how close a shave he'd had with death had set in. "Can you help me please?" he gasped to the RAF military guard on duty.

The guard approached him with extreme caution. "Halt!" he commanded in English. "Stamata!" in Greek and "Dur!" in Turkish.

"Face the wall and put your hands up you filthy Greek terrorist!" he ordered.

Andrew felt the gun barrel press firmly into his back. Oh, no, no! Had he escaped the two gunmen only to be mistaken for a terrorist and be shot by this guard?

Desperately he yelled out as loud as he was able, "I am English. Please I am English! I am not a terrorist. I have just managed to escape from two of them though!"

The guard, still unrelenting pressed the gun even firmer between Andrew's shoulder blades. "You speak good English." he observed.

"That's because I am bloody English," yelled Andrew in utter desperation.

"What did you say?" questioned the guard.

"I said, that's because I am bloody English!" repeated Andrew exasperated, almost falling to his knees.

"Hang on ... is that a Newcastle accent?" quizzed the guard while easing the pressure from his weapon.

"Yes! My home is in Gosforth," Andrew sighed in relief as the gun left his back, "and I'm propa paggered man! Please help me."

"Whey aye man. Areet bonny lad. Wow! I'm from Wallsend. I know Gosforth very well, my uncle lives there. Come in lad and let's get you a bacon butty and a mug of tea. I'm just having one and you can tell me what you are doing here. What's your name?"

"Thanks, am clamming! I'm Andrew Brown a detective from Brighton Police Station, England."

"Let's see your ID card then - just for the record."

Over a welcome cuppa Andrew explained how he had been forcefully abducted from his room at the Holiday Inn in Nicosia and as he struggled in vein with two armed men had managed to kick both his wallet holding his ID and his mobile under the bed. He hoped his DCI would spot them and realise he was in trouble.

He briefly explained they were working on a murder case in England and following leads in Cyprus.

"Crikey! Sounds as though you were lucky to escape! I'm Bert by the way. When you have finished your tea I will take you to my superintendent, Alan Groves."

"Thanks Bert that's fine - and the best bacon butty I've had in a long time!" enthused Andrew wholeheartedly. "And sorry I swore at you."

Bert smiled back and patted him understandingly on the back. "I know what ye be uptee the neet man - sleeping!"

When they arrived at the Superintendent's office Bert explained that morning's events. Andrew collaborated all the facts leading Alan Groves to pose the question, "How on earth could this happen here?"

"I have no idea Sir," answered Andrew. "The last twenty four hours have been something of a maelstrom for me and I'm still trying to come to terms with it all myself.

Could you please phone the Police HQ at Nicosia and ask for Chief Yiannis Galanis?"

"Yes, of course Andrew."

Chapter 8

A feast for the eyes!

"Yes, sorry, but I am so emotional - your Mr Andrew has been found alive," blurted Chief Galanis's secretary excitedly. Harry fell back in his chair, and breathed again, elated.

Chief Galanis took the call from Alan Groves and put it on loud speaker.

"This is Alan Groves. I'm the senior superintendent of the military police at the RAF Radar Installation, Troodos. We have a Mr Andrew Brown here. Apparently he has no identification on him as he kicked it all under his bed in the hotel room. He claims he is a UK police detective. Can you vouch for him and confirm this to be correct Chief Galanis?"

"Yes, of course," shouted out Harry in utter relief. "He came here with me only yesterday. Please tell him we will be up there to collect him as soon as possible. Thank you so much for calling. We have police out searching for him. How is he?"

"He has been roughed up a fair bit but is otherwise alright Sir and is now in good spirits. We are looking after him. We are taking him down for our medical staff to check him over shortly. It was lucky for him he found us. He must have been running flat out for over six miles. He purposely took a zig zag course to us to confuse anyone who may be following him.

At first our man at the gate thought he was a Greek terrorist then recognised his Newcastle accent and brought him to my office. I will tell him you are on your way. Please ask for me when you get to the gate and I will authorise the guard on duty to let you through."

"Okay Harry," sighed Chief Galanis in utter relief. "You can come with me and we will take a second car with us. It's quite a trek up to the Troodos mountains. Have you been there before?"

"Yes Sir, I have some years ago while on holiday. From what I have read the RAF Mount Olympus Radar Station is very high up. How far is it from Nicosia Sir?"

"It's exactly 53 miles and an arduous journey. It will take about 1hour 40minutes."

As they left Harry put a reassuring call through to Angela explaining they were on their way to pick up Andrew.

They made good progress on the journey. The Cypriot police were used to driving over the rough mountainous terrain and didn't spare the horses! Harry was anxious as to how Andrew was and hoped he wouldn't be too adversely effected mentally by the events of the last 24 hours.

Soon the radar station was filling the horizon belittling the lush pine forest and everything else in it's wake. At the main gate the military police stopped their cars. Chief Galanis asked to see Superintendent Alan Groves.

"No problem Sir, he is expecting you," and he waved both cars through.

Alan Groves met them outside and took them through a side entrance.

"This is a top secret Radar area so we have to keep you away from the main radar area," he explained.

"Here we are, my office," ... he threw the door wide open and stood back ... "and this gentleman is your man, Andrew Brown!"

Harry immediately clasped Andrew in a huge bear hug and was loath to let him go. "You are a feast for the eyes Andrew! Thank God you are safe!"

"Yes it has been an experience I will never forget Harry - but I am fine now just a bit sore and tired. The two men who abducted me are an evil lot. We must be very weary of them in the future. Given a gun I wouldn't hesitate in pulling the trigger!"

"I'm sure you feel that way Andrew. I understand."

"Right Andrew," added Chief Galanis, "let's get you back to the station and if you can please give us a full report. I will arrange for a search over a 6 mile area and we can try to establish just where you were held."

On the journey back Andrew slept like a baby sprawled over the back seat. Back at Police HQ Harry gave the now wide awake Andrew his wallet and phone back.

"Thanks Harry. I managed to kick them under the bed, I thought you would find them there."

"Okay Andrew, I'll have a strong coffee, I'll get you a large cool Coke and I will record your report on my phone." Chief Galanis was fine with that.

Harry announced into his phone, "Andrew's report."

"Right Harry, when we returned from the restaurant we changed rooms. You took my room and I took your room number 412. I had just started to unpack when ...

...
...
...
...
...
...
...
...
...
...
...
...

... then Bert took me in for a cuppa and a bacon butty, and well, you know the rest."

"One more thing," interrupted Chief Galanis. "Can you give me a full description of the men please?"

"Yes, of course Sir. It was the middle of the night and the light was not good inside. I was also woozy from the roughing up they gave me but here goes ... One is unshaven, black haired about 5'10", of medium build and pugnacious in both manner and appearance to the nth degree. Probably in his 40's. The other one younger, a more nervous character with long ginger hair and about 6' tall."

"Thank you Andrew. I suggest you and Harry go back to the Holiday Inn and stay in tonight. I will arrange for a car to take you there and to pick you up again at 9am. I will have a police officer on duty at the hotel the entire night.

Hopefully they will not try anything again. The police officer on guard will be a safe deterrent though," he smiled reassuringly.

Chapter 9

Curiouser and Curiouser

"We checked out the address your DCS Street gave us for Mr Dimitris Pantazis Harry, it's 1468 Arios Antonios, Nicosia. It is unoccupied so following further investigations we discovered he also stays in a luxury villa overlooking the sea.

It's not that far from Limassol ... so tomorrow we are going out to look at this villa. It's in Amathus a Limassol district. There is also a lady living there with her daughter who we should question."

"That's it!" exclaimed Harry. "In the photo we found, the Troodos mountains are in the background. Our mystery lady diner maybe! Andrew show Chief Galanis the photo from The Grand's restaurant that you obtained from the CCTV camera and the one we found in the safe, Angie S."

"Yes Andrew, that could well be her," confirmed Yiannis Galanis. "As I said, she has her daughter living with her too. Tomorrow we must be on our guard though as it's just possible there could be armed men around. Is there anything else we could help you both with Harry?"

"Yes. I would like to visit the Nicosia Bank to ask about their vaults and to check out a safety deposit box. It would be most helpful if you could be present for this too Sir?"

"Of course, not a problem Harry. I will be with you as often as I possibly can be. I might find it very interesting and informative accompanying you both," Chief Galanis smiled warmly at them.

"One thing I am curious about though, is how could the two men come to abduct Andrew from the Holiday Inn almost immediately after you arrived in Cyprus? Who fed them the information they required like the flight you were catching, the hotel you were staying at and your room number? Curiouser and curiouser as your Lewis Carroll's Alice might say!"

"Indeed Sir," smiled Harry, the analogy tickling him somewhat. He did not see Chief Yiannis Galanis as an Alice fan - or the Holiday Inn as Wonderland come to that!

"I don't know the answers to that for sure Sir, but it is concerning," agreed Harry, "so I will call our DCS this evening and ask him to check something out for me. If I am right it could be very serious indeed."

"Okay. I will await with interest. Your car is now outside, antio sas, goodbye and have a good rest Andrew. We will see you both in the morning."

Back at the Holiday Inn the two police officers confirmed one of them would remain on guard throughout the night from 10pm onwards.

"Efcharisto, thanks," replied Harry.

"Antio - sas, goodbye," one of the officers smiled back.

On their way through reception, Harry suggested they ask for another room adjoining 412. The reception manager was most obliging and offered room 413. They took it.

"Okay Andrew, let's go up and sort out our clothes. Give me a knock when you have rested sufficiently and we will head down to the restaurant for a well deserved dinner!"

"Great Harry, I'm happy with that, I could eat a horse! I see they have fitted you out with a bullet proof vest and gun?"

"Yes, Chief Galanis took me down to the armoury earlier on and he is getting you fitted out tomorrow."

"Oh, that's a huge relief! I will feel more comfortable with protection - especially with a gun - just wish I'd had one yesterday! Those two men are animals Harry. They're highly dangerous and do not give a fig for human life. Apart from their own that is."

"Yes Andrew and it is for that very reason we must stick closely together whenever we are out and remain ultra vigilant at all times," Harry impressed firmly on the young detective beside him.

"Right, here we are! See you later."

Harry walked on round to the small room at the back to collect his holdall. After he'd unpacked his gear in room 413 he decided to email the day's official report to Angela then followed up with a call updating her on Andrew's well-being. He knew she would be worrying.

"Please take good care of him Harry."

"No problem. I'm in the room next door now! I have a hunch during the next few days we will be needing and looking after each other's backs constantly.

How did you get on with your enquiries regarding Eugene the waiter at the Ship Hotel Angela?"

"Very well Harry. His surname is Demirci and he is a Turkish Cypriot. He travels out to Cyprus three or four times a year, staying at Famagusta and in the northern half of Nicosia.

One other thing I have to tell you. The post-mortem has been completed on Mr Dimitris Pantazis and his body is being flown out to Cyprus for repatriation within the next couple of days. I will keep you updated on that one."

"Thanks Angela, if I'm not pushing my luck here could you please just find out more on Mr Clive Bowman, Winnie's brother in law. That would be of great help."

"No problem Harry," she laughed, "I will soon qualify for your job at this rate! So, what are you planning next?"

"Well, the Chief of Police here, Yiannis Galanis is taking us to Amathus near Limassol tomorrow to the villa where Angie S lives. We have to question her about her relationship with Dimitris Pantazis. I must add though Angela, Chief Galanis is looking after us really well and was genuinely concerned and helpful when Andrew was abducted."

"That's good to know as the DCS really rates him too. So what will you ask the mysterious Angie S?"

"Primarily as I said, her relationship with Mr Pantazis; her nationality; does she travel to England frequently if so for what reason and is it primarily to Brighton?

I hope she will be cooperative but uppermost in my thoughts, I hope we do not get hijacked by those two mad gunmen. The roads are extremely remote. Chief Galanis will have us both fitted out with vests and guns by then though for such an eventuality as he too is genuinely concerned for our welfare.

The following day he is taking us to the bank of Nicosia. I want to check the number I deciphered from the back of the gold Rolex we found among Mr Pantazis's possessions. We may encounter a problem actually getting inside the vault however as I believe they have face recognition, but we can hopefully sort that out on the day."

"Gosh, you do have a full itinerary! Keep me informed here Harry and please don't take unnecessary chances!"

"Would I mum?" he chuckled, "Would I?"

"Cheeky Monkey!"

"I'll text you a report."

One of the Cypriot officers who took them back to the Holiday Inn confirmed he would stay on duty until midnight protecting them when a fellow officer would relieve him. Harry thanked him, admitting they would feel safer with an armed guard.

"We will just freshen up, take a leisurely meal then have an early night."

"Fine. You will see me around. I will be taking you to the station for your 9am appointment with Chief Galanis. He will then be taking you both on to Amathus."

Harry and Andrew chose simple meals of chicken salad and steak and chips respectively then apple pie with vanilla sauce for dessert.

On their way to the lift they passed their friendly guard. "Kalinychta," Harry smiled.

"Goodnight," grinned the guard.

As they reached their rooms Andrew beamed, "Kalinychta."

"You too Andrew. I will call you around 7.30 in the morning to go down for breakfast. Now, catch up on some much needed sleep."

Bang on 7.30 Andrew's phone rang. "Kalimera Harry," he chirped. "I've had the sleep of my life - just need a quick shower now before breakfast."

"That's great Andrew ... did you swallow a Greek dictionary or are you just learning the language in your sleep?" he laughed.

The two officers were waiting for them in Reception after breakfast and asked if they were ready to go.

"Yes, we are thanks. Efharisto."

Chief Galanis was there to greet them at the station.

"He's looking chuffed," whispered Andrew to Harry, "maybe he has good news?"

"Firstly, I am pleased you are looking so well now Andrew. I trust you had a good night's sleep?"

"Indeed Sir, and raring to go for my morning run!"

"Oh No! No, no, no Andrew! Not yet, I am sorry. Well gentlemen, my officers have been checking out our Mr Pantazis and we can tell you this:

He was divorced about five years ago.

His ex wife's name is Thalia.

They have two children, twin boys Georgios and Xanda.

Thalia has applied to the UK authorities to have Dimitris Pantazis repatriated here soon.

She is arranging a funeral service and burial at the St George Orthodox Church, Lefkosia.

For the last four years Mr Pantazis has let out his house as a holiday home with the full agreement of his ex wife.

Thalia did not want it sold as she thought it would be security later for the two boys.

He has been living at the villa in Amathus while in Cyprus.

He travelled regularly to England and Turkey.

The villa belongs to a Mrs Angie Sakalis. She has one daughter aged around 24.

The daughter is home now for the summer but most of the year she is at university in the UK. One interesting nugget of information - Mrs Sakalis has a large, luxury apartment in Brighton, one of four overlooking the pier. I have asked your DCS John Street to check out the address.

We do have a business address for Mr Pantazis near Larnaca. It is being checked out as we speak. He once had a business partner a Mr Nico Castellanos. DCS Street explained you found out from your investigations this man had cancelled a trip to England just after Mr Pantazis was shot."

"Yes, that's correct Sir. So their business was diamonds?"

"Yes Harry. We are making checks on Mr Pantazis's bank details also trying to establish where Nico Castellanos is holed up now. I will keep you updated on incoming information as and when we receive it" Harry nodded in appreciation.

"Before we leave one of my officers will take Andrew down to the armoury."

Andrew's face lit up as he was keen to know what type of gun it would be. Chief Galanis explained they were all issued with a Smith and Wesson automatic.

While they were down in the armoury Harry took a call from Angela. She had found the address of Mrs Sakalis's Brighton apartment, so he updated Yiannis Galanis and Andrew when they returned.

Information now seemed to be flooding in thick and fast. The Chief received a call from the Manager of the Holiday Inn. She confirmed one of the receptionists took a call from a lady in England a couple of evenings ago asking to speak to Harry Webb and requesting his room number. She also wanted to know whether it was overlooking Metaxas Square.

Unfortunately the trainee receptionist happily gave her all the information she had requested.

Chief Galanis was very angry at this breach of confidentiality so freely given and demanded it should never happen in the future.

"Could it have been your Liz?" Andrew asked Harry.

"No. She wouldn't do that Andrew, but I will check of course. If not we really do need to establish who this lady caller actually was."

Chapter 10

La Gioconda

"**R**ight, let's be on our way to Amathus. We're all armed and wearing protective vests but please still remain alert during the journey," Chief Galanis warned. "If Mrs Sakalis is at home we will probably glean more information from her. Both of you travel in my car please and there will be another police vehicle following closely behind. I am extremely mindful of keeping you both safe!"*

The journey to Amathus took 90 minutes. En route Chief Galanis was most interested in the murder investigations taking place in Brighton and was especially intrigued with bags of diamonds being hidden behind the MGBs' radios.

"I am enlightened!" he exclaimed. "So clever finding them Harry!"

"Right, this is the place, Villa Alexelio, Amathus, Limassol District, 4533. Yes?" The driver nodded.

As they pulled into the drive Andrew was transfixed by the beautiful position in which the villa was set and with good reason. It bordered the sea and boasted immaculately manicured gardens. Watte or mimosa trees surrounded the windows in a magnificent cloud of yellow which looked quite stunning against the electric blue paintwork.

The sound of the hummingbirds gently thrummed through the hot, scented air which added to the wonder of the Troodos mountains standing so proud and magnificent beyond the blue tiled swimming pool.

As they approached the front door a very attractive lady asked if she could help them. She was dressed in a pure white dress of cooling lawn cotton which draped oh so beautifully over her shoulders and chest, not unlike a Grecian goddess. Delicate white strapped sandals with the merest touch of gold complemented it delightfully. She wore no jewellery apart from a stunning gold Rolex watch.

Just like Leonardo's La Gioconda she needed no embellishments around her neck.

Harry was the first to speak and he introduced himself, his assistant detective Andrew Brown and Chief Yiannis Galanis of the Nicosia police, explaining they were investigating the murder of Mr Dimitris Pantazis in Brighton.

"Are you Mrs Angie Sakalis?" he asked.

"Yes," she replied as she visibly welled up, "please come in."

As they walked through to the conservatory another young lady appeared. "Mum, is anything wrong?" she asked.

"It's okay Chloe. These men are detectives from England and they are accompanied by Police Chief Galanis from Nicosia."

"Oh, I will make a jug of fresh iced fruit juice. I expect everyone would like a glass?"

"Thank you Chloe."

Chloe had a dainty slim body, dimpled shoulders, vibrant eyes and glowing young skin, all well complemented by her scanty bright pink bikini and peacock blue throw. She was filled with a joie de vivre.

"I will help you," volunteered Andrew, looking completely smitten as he followed her out like a faithful puppy dog.

Harry explained to Angie Sakalis why they were there and gave a brief outline of the tragic events in Brighton.

"I would really appreciate from you Mrs Sakalis, full and honest answers to my questions. Firstly, how long have you known Mr Pantazis and did he ever stay with you in your apartment in Brighton?"

"Well, I have known Dimitris for probably over ten years. He was in business with my husband Nicholas you see. We were always very good friends with both Dimitris and Thalia and spent many lovely holidays with them.

Whenever Dimitris was in Brighton he used to stay with us in our apartment and would park his car in our underground parking lot."

"Oh, that's interesting! Just two days before he was shot on Brighton beach he stayed at The Grand and parked his MGB in the carpark at Brunswick parking. Why do you think that was?"

"Yes, that's correct. I had a flight booked from Gatwick early in the morning to Larnaca. I had let the apartment out for two months so Dimitris said he would book into The Grand. We later had dinner together there."

"Yes, we did see you both on the hotel's CCTV."

Mrs Sakalis became very tearful once more, "I'm so sorry Mrs Sakalis but this line of enquiry is crucial to our investigation. I do hope you understand," consoled Harry.

Just then Chloe appeared with a welcoming tray of iced drinks followed by Andrew who gave Harry a discreet little wink.

Chloe put a protective arm around her mother.

"Where is your husband now Mrs Sakalis?"

"I can tell you about my father," Chloe offered. "He died four years ago when his car went over the cliff edge on the Troodos mountain road. It was stated in evidence at the inquest that he drove into another car, swerved violently to the right, lost control and failed to stop.

My mother and I did not agree with this 'evidence', however. We believe to this day the two men in the car stage managed his murder and pushed his car over the edge."

Chloe turned to Chief Galanis and suggested he looked back at the case file.

"Yes, of course Chloe. I remember it well. I had just arrived from Athens to take over this new post in Nicosia. I had been told your father's case was closed but I will certainly reopen it when I return."

Harry could only sympathise and admitted Chloe's account sounded very plausible. The thought also crossed his mind it could be the same two thugs they were after.

"You mentioned your husband and Mr Pantazis were in business together. What business was that?"

"Oh, we were all four business partners in a chain of high-end jewellery shops in the West End of London, Cyprus and Turkey. The shops have all been sold now however and with the proceeds we invested in two hotels in Coral Bay, Paphos. I own this villa and the luxury apartment in Brighton.

Also we still have connections with the diamond trade and do a few private sales both here and abroad. That's why

Dimitris was in Brighton I believe - executing a one off cash transaction."

"Had you been married long Mrs Sakalis?"

She once again was overcome with grief. "Actually yes, it would have been 26 years next month."

"Yes, and it's my 25th birthday!" Chloe volunteered.

"That's right Chloe but sadly there will not be your father or Dimitris to celebrate it with you."

"Don't worry mum, Thalia and the twins are coming to my party."

"Could we have Thalia's phone number please?" asked Harry. "Have you known her for a long time?"

"Oh, yes Sir. We were both hostesses on the Cyprus airline flights and coincidentally we both met our husbands on their business trips, so ummm, quite a long time," she reflected with obvious fond memories and emotions. Harry smiled comfortingly at her.

"Chloe would you please give Andrew Thalia's number?"

Chief Galanis then asked why the house in Nicosia, 1465 Arios, Antonios was unoccupied.

"It has been for the past four weeks as it's being redecorated ready for the next two year let."

"Thank you Mrs Sakalis."

Harry was obviously deep in one of his reveries before questioning, "There is just one other man we would like some information about, a Mr Nico Castellanos. Could you tell me about him and where he lives please?"

At the mention of the name Nico Castellanos Angie Sakalis jumped to her feet in rage and turned red faced.

"Please, I am so angry with that ... with that ... man!!" she sobbed. "Initially and for many years we always thought him to be a good man and business partner but then he seemed to get mixed up with a bad lot and tried to steal our business. He even threatened to take our lives!"

"Again, if you check your records," Chloe interrupted, aiming her remarks to Chief Galanis, "you will find many reports of my mother's complaints and worries about him. I am certain he has two dangerous men working on his behalf, doing his dirty work, in both Cyprus and England."

Harry and Andrew threw each other glances of amazement. Could another major part of this puzzle be slotting into place at last?

"Andrew show Mrs Sakalis the photo of the man at The Grand," asked Harry as he discreetly pointed to his hair.

Andrew took out his phone. "Is this Nico Castellanos Mrs Sakalis?" Andrew asked. "He has a white streak in his hair."

"Yes, that's him! We never want to see him again!"

"I think enough questions for today," Chloe insisted, being very protective of her mum, "but if you would like to come back again we will help you as much as we possibly can."

Andrew smiled back at her tenderly. "Yes, thank you Chloe and thank you Mrs Sakalis, we may have to. Antio sas!" Andrew added, hoping it would not be a long 'goodbye'.

Back in the car Harry demanded, "Come on then Andrew. What information did you manage to get from young Chloe? You were certainly a long time making those drinks!"

"Yes Harry, she has sunshine in her soul doesn't she? We hit it off right away. I was absolutely delighted when she told me she is studying at Oxford University and taking her degree in Criminology.

She is on a case study at the London Metropolitan. We have exchanged emails and will meet up in London when she is back in Oxford. We just seem to 'fit' perfectly Harry like a hand in a kid leather glove. We will both be following a similar career path too. Absolutely perfect. She has a flat in Hammersmith and when her mum is in Brighton she stays with her."

"That is such good news Andrew I could tell you were smitten from the moment you first meet her! The fact is I have never seen you so 'ogle eyed' I believe is the expression. What say you Chief?"

"Ah yes, young love!" exclaimed Chief Galanis, "let me quote for you ...

'Shall I compare thee to a summer's day?

Thou art more lovely and more temperate.

Rough winds do shake the darling buds of May

And summer's lease has all too short a date ...'"

"Shakespeare," smiled Harry at Chief Galanis.

"William Shakespeare indeed Harry! Sonnet number 18. He's almost as good as Lewis Carroll don't you think? And then H.E. Bates claimed one line of course for his Larkin books."

Harry looked over at Andrew and they both chuckled silently.

"Quite an earth shattering experience you've had in your first few days here Andrew. Those awful thugs abducting you and beating you up when you first arrived then young Chloe Sakalis appearing from nowhere and knocking you for six!" The chief laughed heartily at his own little joke.

He then put a call back to the police station and his jovial mood changed dramatically. He was shouting at the top of his voice demanding a full report by the end of the day regarding the incident on the Troodos mountains where Chloe's dad's car went over the steep edge. Harry could pick up much of the conversation but not the finer details.

Galanis also demanded all reports from Limassol Police on the complaints regarding Nico Castellanos be on his desk ready for his return. Also had this man left Cyprus recently and if so where did he go? Had anyone else left with him? All reports and answers should be on his desk ready and waiting for his imminent return.

The final call he made was to the bank of Cyprus in Nicosia where he spoke to the bank manager and arranged for Harry and Andrew, accompanied by himself, to take a look in their vault the next day at 10.30am.

Harry and Andrew meanwhile were discussing the information on Mr Nico Castellanos.

"All this explains why he had a heated meeting with Mr Pantazis in The Grand but why did he use the pseudonym 'Bert Barber' with Max Grey? Did he have a secret to hide from him? He even went to the trouble of having business cards printed using the fake ID?" added Andrew.

"Yes, he was certainly keeping his real name a secret from Max Grey. We must find out why. But on our visit to the Sakalis's home today we had a trio of breakthroughs. I just love it when suddenly three pieces of the jigsaw slot into place Andrew!" exclaimed Harry.

"Just this rather odd irregular one about the man's name or names rather ... but I don't think it's too relevant to us. It could be to Max Grey though!"

Very soon they arrived at the Nicosia Police Station. Galanis hopped out of the vehicle almost before it had stopped like a man on a mission.

"Right, those reports had better be waiting!"

They all followed close on his heels to his office where the reports were dutifully stacked on his desk.

"Right, let's look at the car accident from four years ago first ... Well Mrs Sakalis was correct, she did ask for further investigations as she wasn't at all convinced her husband was at fault. From the start she maintained he was deliberately pushed over the edge.

... No other witnesses though other cars did pass by, saw his car go over then called the police and ambulance services.

The two men in the other car insisted however Mr Sakalis had hit their car, turned over and dropped over the precipice. Unfortunately, probably preplanned and orchestrated, it was in an area where the safety barrier was broken.

Here is the statement Harry. It's the two men you have been after, Mr Yirgos Papadopoulos and Mr Andreas Athanasiou. What do you make of that?"

"I believe Mrs Sakalis was right. It is just what those two men would do. They are killers and need to be apprehended urgently."

"We have my men searching the Troodos area now so hopefully we will find them soon," Chief Galanis assured Harry.

"Here is the report from Limassol police concerning Mrs Sakalis's complaints on Mr Nico Castellanos. I will have a few stern words with them on why her calls were not taken seriously.

... Ah, and this is a passenger list of flights to Turkey. Our Nico Castellanos is listed as boarding one just two days before you arrived. That is most unfortunate as you know Harry, the Turkish police will not help us I'm afraid. So, I suggest you both return to the Holiday Inn, with a police guard of course. It has been a long day. I will send a car to collect you in the morning to take you to the Cyprus Bank."

"Fine Sir," Harry acknowledged.

"Antio-sas," replied Andrew.

Chief Galanis smiled his goodbye.

On their journey back to the hotel Harry asked the two police officers accompanying them if they could all go out that evening for a dinner in the Nando's restaurant in Soloman Square. They checked with their chief who thought it would be fine as long as they all ate together and were back in their rooms before 11pm.

Both police officers spoke very good English which helped the evening to go well.

Harry had thought Andrew would appreciate an evening out at a familiar eatery - and he did. He was in his element explaining to them all that the Nando's chain had a total of 913 outlets, three of those being in his home city of Newcastle, which incidentally he visited often while he was home!

The two police officers seemed really interested in Andrew's enthusiasm about the place - unless of course they were just being polite - even when he further went on to explain the chain was actually started in Johannesburg, South Africa in 1987 ...

Harry smiled inwardly as Andrew's tensions of the previous two days dissipated before his eyes.

The two officers then politely asked Harry about his home town and London. They both wanted to travel to England soon and asked of places they should visit. Harry suggested Bath, the Midlands, Wales, Scotland and Ireland, to which Andrew piped up, "Don't forget Newcastle!"

The waiter who had been hovering patiently for a break in the conversation finally had the chance to explain the special tonight was the popular Pino Pittas. These were flame grilled chicken thighs served with grilled halloumi and caramelised red onion relish.

"Yes!" Exclaimed Andrew with gusto, so it was four of those with three Keos and a Coke. Two 'Choc a Lot' cakes were later devoured by the officers, two 'Gogey Caramel Cheesecakes by Harry and Andrew with another round of drinks.

"Do you enjoy working for Chief Galanis?" Harry asked the officers.

"Yes, he is demanding but very good to us and takes incredible interest in his cases. He is very thorough and his results without fail substantiate this."

The evening was a great success and Harry thanked the officers for joining them. They in turn confirmed they would take it in turns to keep guard through the night and would then take them to the police station at 9am after breakfast.

"Have a good night Andrew and see you about 7.45am."

"Yamas," replied Andrew.

Harry laughed, "You are getting good at the language Andrew. I will just send an update email to Angela then she will have a copy on the DCS's desk before we start in the morning, taking the time difference into account that is."

⸻⟨⟩⸻

Chapter 11

How long is forever? Sometimes, just one second!

During breakfast the two of them discussed what might happen when they arrived at the bank. 'What would the safety deposit box hold?' was the main topic of conversation.

"Well Andrew I have in my head three possibilities. One - it could be empty; two - it could be full of euros or three - maybe it's full of diamonds!

I just hope I have decrypted the code correctly for opening the thing because if not they have no conventional locks so we could be scuppered from the onset."

"No special keys then Harry?"

"Not for this Andrew, no."

"I have faith in you Harry."

The police guards ambled over to their table and joined them for coffee. They both politely thanked the two Englishmen for a most enjoyable evening yesterday.

As they downed their last sips of espresso Harry checked his watch and reluctantly suggested they take their leave as they didn't want to keep Chief Galanis waiting.

By the time they arrived at the police station he was ready to go and after a brief enquiry as to whether their evening was a success he exclaimed, "Okay, let's see what this bank vault has to offer."

It didn't seem long before the driver was dropping them off at the impressive front door of the Nicosia Bank before parking up the car at the rear.

At reception Galanis asked the receptionist to see the manager, Mr Andrew Kokkinides, as they had an appointment with him at 10.30am.

"Kalimera Sir, if you would follow me please I will take you to his office." She knocked on his door before opening it, "Three visitors to see you Sir. Your 10.30 appointment."

"Thank you," he acknowledged then turning to the three men announced, "I will take you down to the bank vaults now. You said you wanted to look at the late Mr Dimitris Pantazis's safe deposit box?"

"Yes please."

On the way down he resumed his conversation ...

"He was a very good customer for many years and of course his ex wife Mrs Thalia Pantazis is still a most valued customer of ours."

As they arrived at the vault door Mr Kokkinides buzzed in a code and the vault door opened. Harry asked if the safe deposit codes were 5 or 6 digits with a combination of letters and numbers.

"Yes, most of our customers use the 6 digit format. I do not have any information on any of the safe codes of course as they are kept secret by my customers. Even if I had any information Sir, unfortunately I would not be able to divulge it to a third party.

"I was a little concerned you may just have facial recognition here," Harry confided in Mr Kokkinides.

"No, it's not mandatory. We do indeed have facial recognition for those customers who specify they prefer it, but no, it is not a blanket requisite here."

"Well, I must confess that is a huge relief to us Sir."

"Mr Pantazis's safety deposit box is located on the second level. The last one on the right, just over there he gesticulated. I will leave you now but I will have to close the door. Just use the buzzer on the right when your business is done then I will open the door for you."

They all looked at the safety deposit box in anticipation before Chief Galanis announced, "Right Harry, let's see what you can do."

Harry, rather nervously for him, stepped up to the plate. "Well I must pre-warn you this could take forever!"

"How long is forever? Sometimes, just one second!" Galanis quoted.

"Lewis Carroll?" asked Andrew smiling.

Galanis nodded.

Harry took a deep breath in. "Well, I will try this one first. It seems the easiest but for that reason the least likely." He typed in ...

... s500xm ...

Nothing happened.

"Diddly squat," announced Andrew dejectedly.

149

Galanis looked at him completely bewildered. It certainly wasn't a Lewis Carroll quote he mused.

Harry consulted his notepad which held umpteen workings out. "This one I think I have most faith in ...

... mlod7x ... "

Nothing happened.

Harry consulted his note pad again as he ran his fingers urgently through his hair. A habit he often deployed Andrew had noticed from previous experiences when he became a little perplexed or needed to reboot his brain ... but it always seemed to produce the required results ...

"Got it!!" He suddenly exclaimed. "I need to turn it upside down and back to front! So it now reads ...

... xLpolw ... "

The door clicked open. Andrew punched the air in sheer delight - he had every faith in his mentor.

"Oh Harry! You didn't work on Colossus at Bletchley Park in a pervious lifetime by any chance did you?"

Harry beamed. He was both relieved and delighted.

"Oh! Wouldn't that have been great Andrew! Working in Alan Turing's team when they eventually broke the Enigma code? I have visited there a few times, entered the office he worked in, was given a fantastic talk by staff on both the Enigma and Colossus and you can even try your hand at decoding yourself. Easy ones of course!"

"Well, to you maybe!"

Refocusing, they could see the box was absolutely full to the brim, literally dripping with bags of diamonds.

Galanis was most impressed, "Well done Harry! I don't know how your grey matter came up with that combination my man but you were absolutely brilliant. How do you do it?"

"Oh, just through years of experience Sir," Harry smiled modestly though inwardly swelling with pride and giving himself a hearty pat on the back.

Suddenly though their attention was diverted to Andrew who was breaking into a cold sweat and standing rigid on the floor of the vault, his face as white as Mrs Sakalis's lawn cotton dress.

"Andrew, what's the matter my boy?" asked Galanis deeply concerned as he went over and grasped his arm.

"Claustrophobia. Quick! Please get me out of here now," he begged as he tried to gulp in lungfuls of air.

Harry immediately closed the safe door and scrambled the combination as Galanis pressed the door buzzer. Mr Kokkinides thankfully opened up right away and Andrew pushed his way out ahead of the others.

Harry and Chief Galanis thanked Mr Kokkinides. They explained they would be talking to Mrs Pantazis soon who would be in touch with him regarding the contents of the safe.

"Well yes Sir. It has certainly been very upsetting for Mrs Pantazis and the twins, also for Mrs Sakalis and her daughter."

"Do you know them all Sir?" asked Harry.

"Yes Sir, they are my best customers. I have just received a call from Mrs Pantazis in fact informing me Dimitris Pantazis's body was flown in last night and his funeral is tomorrow at 1pm."

"Did she tell you where Sir?"

"Yes. It will be at the St George Orthodox Church in Lefkosia. I will be attending."

"Well thank you once again Mr Kokkinides, we may need to come back but if so we will make an appointment with you. Antio-sas"

"Goodbye."

Harry had a quick word with Andrew who was fine now out in the fresh open air.

"Let's get back to the police station and see what further information we can find out about tomorrow's funeral," briefed Galanis. "I think we should all go to pay our respects but maintain a discreet distance in the background."

"Yes Sir," agreed Harry.

"Andrew could you email today's events and tomorrow's plans to Angela ASAP."

"I'm on it."

Chapter 12

'Stop all the clocks, cut off the telephone'
Prevent the dog from barking with a juicy bone,
Silence the pianos and with muffled drum,
Bring out the coffin, let the mourners come...

*A*t the police station Chief Galanis phoned the Presbyter Leronymos at the St George Church to obtain permission for the three of them to attend the following day's funeral service for Mr Dimitris Pantazis.

He agreed with the proviso, according to local protocol, they take the rear row of seats inside the church.

"So my two English detectives, let's discuss our next move. What are your thoughts Harry?"

"I think we must speak to Mrs Thalia Pantazis at the church tomorrow to arrange a meeting for the following day. We also need to speak to Mrs Angie Sakalis again.

Just, maybe, they could enlighten us regarding the diamonds in the safe deposit box and the two bags of diamonds in our safe at Brighton Police Station. It will be interesting to see who assumes ownership or perhaps they may plan on splitting the spoils 50/50.

Then of course there is the case of euros, the Rolex watch and Mr Pantazis's expensive suits and shirts. I don't think we should mention the gun just yet."

"I agree Harry but our absolute top priority should be locating those two murdering thugs," declared Galanis with venom.

"By my reckoning Sir they must be holed up near the green line border, maybe still at the same place they held Andrew. Any news on them by your men who are searching the area?"

"Yes, still very sketchy at the moment but apparently they have been sighted a few times in the said vicinity so my officers are following up a few leads as we speak."

"Oh! Brilliant news. Let's hope we capture them both soon!" Harry sighed in both relief and anticipation.

"And of course when we return to Brighton we still have many loose ends to tie up there:

1) Who was the lady who telephoned the Holiday Inn here asking the number of my room?

2) Could she be the 'mastermind' back in Brighton and if so are we already aware of her?

Personally I am very wary and suspicious of Max's wife, Jane Grey. 'Why?' You may well ask. Well, I could not tell you specifically. I have no tangible reason whatsoever … it's just the way she sits in on our conversations, listening intently without ever speaking a word, blending herself into the background like a chameleon, taking in all that is said but revealing nothing …

That unnerves me somewhat. Still waters often run deep in my opinion.

Winnie Williams herself is an enigma too - why on earth would she have Mr Pantazis in her personal address book? It does not make sense!

So, onto the men. There is the hotel waiter, Eugene. He knew Winnie, though just casually we are lead to believe. We have discovered he is part Turkish but he emphatically doesn't want to talk about that. Why?

Also why would our secretive waiter miss a day's pay to attend a random customer's funeral? Answers on the back of a postage stamp please gentlemen!

Oh, yes! Now Linda's husband, Clive Bowman who has tenuous links with the units at Gatwick. He also knows many of the people we have come to know during these enquiries. The mind I'm afraid boggles! Absolutely blooming boggles!

So, all the aforementioned are appetising foods for thought, but we still have much to tie up here first and foremost as you say. We are all in full agreement catching those two thugs must be top of the agenda right now."

"Here, here Harry. I have two guards waiting now to take you both back to the Holiday Inn and they will continue to stay with you for as many nights as it takes until we catch those two gunmen.

As the funeral isn't until 1pm tomorrow just have a restful early morning, catch up on your correspondence and the car will pick you up at 11.45."

"Thank you Sir, yamas," replied Andrew. "Any chance I could go for a run yet? I have all this pent up energy pounding through my veins, struggling in earnest to escape!"

"Certainly not Andrew! It is not safe, besides which my officers would not be able to keep up with you."

Back at the hotel Harry suggested they have a quick dinner and a drink in the hotel bar before retiring.

Next morning he knocked for Andrew at 8am on the way down to breakfast Andrew announced he had rung his parents earlier.

"Did you tell them anything?"

"Oh no fear! They would not have let me come out to play with you again Harry! They once banned me from seeing my old school pal, Terry Jones, when I was just seven because he accidentally tripped me up in the playground. Horror of horrors I actually grazed my knee you know!

After that I was ordered to mix with nicer boys from good families."

They both broke into spontaneous fits of laughter. "So what became of that thug Terry Jones and his family Andrew, do you know?"

"Oh yes," he responded po-faced, "he is studying to be a doctor; his sister is an Astrophysicist; his father is a High Court Judge and his mother an eminent surgeon at the Royal Victoria Infirmary in Newcastle."

Harry doubled over in fits of laughter, tears rolling down his cheeks. "It's the way you tell it Andrew, so nonchalantly."

Just a few steps further on they encountered one of the guards who was just leaving the breakfast room.

"Kalimera," smiled Andrew.

"Kalimera Mr Andrew ... are you okay Mr Harry?"

Harry nodded as he wiped tears from his eyes.

After breakfast Harry decided he should ring his wife Liz to let her know they were both well; to check whether she was and ask if everything was tickety-boo at home.

"Meanwhile would you put in a call to Angela at the office Andrew? I know we have sent emails and texts but it is only right we touch base occasionally to let her know we are both okay."

"Certainly."

At about 11.30 Harry rapped on Andrew's door. "Right. Let's get down to Reception. The car will be here to pick us up soon. Did you manage to speak with Angela?"

"Yep. We had a good long chat. Everything is fine back at the station and she keeps the DCS fully updated with our emails and texts. She's happy we are both okay but wants us to be extra careful when we do catch up with the two gunmen. I assured her we would be. Did you get a call to Liz Harry?"

"Yes, she too was pleased we were both okay and 'wants us to keep out of trouble'!" Harry smothered another laugh, "As you can guess I didn't explain to her the more dangerous intricacies of work here either.

Consequently she was most concerned about when exactly we would be coming back home from our 'little vacation' as, wait for it, the lawn needs cutting badly!!"

"Yes, sadly our work is not something we can really discuss with our families is it?" Andrew sighed.

"When we get chance though Harry perhaps you will tell me more about how you started in the police force. I have been so intrigued ever since you told me you had been involved in undercover work to the extent of going incognito!"

"Yes I will tell you more about myself later. It could be cathartic actually for both of us to get things off our chests after this operation is done and dusted! Like a sort of pals debriefing session."

Harry looked out of the window, "The car is here Andrew let's go!"

"Kalimera," greeted the driver. "We are picking up the Chief en route."

"Efcharisto," replied Harry.

"That's a new one!" whispered Andrew.

"Just another word for 'thanks'," explained Harry.

At the station Chief Galanis came into the car and assumed his usual position in the front seat.

"Kalimera."

"Kalimera," came a volley of replies.

They arrived at the Orthodox Church just after 12.40. Galanis suggested they go straight in and take their seats at the rear as requested by the Presbyter.

Andrew was amazed at the sheer beauty and opulence of the building; the colossal amount of pillars towering high into the ceiling and the marble tiles that covered the entire floor.

"Yes Andrew," whispered Harry. "I read up about this church. It is over two thousand years old so all the work here was painstakingly undertaken by artisans who took immense pride in their craftsmanship."

The building was quite dark inside and the sheer amount of marble kept it at a comfortably cool temperature.

"Also," informed Harry, "it is traditional for everyone to wear black. Typically the men to wear black suits and women black dresses which cover the legs and arms. This is why we are sitting out of sight in the back row."

The Church was rapidly filling with mourners and soon the Presbyter was at the alter beckoning the congregation to stand.

This signalled the funeral cortège to enter the church. Four solemn coffin bearers wearing identical black suits and large black hats slowly carried the casket down the aisle. They placed it gently before the altar and positioned a religious iconic crown near the deceased's head before gracefully standing back.

They were followed in by Mrs Pantazis and her twin boys Xanda and Georgios. Mrs Pantazis wore a black cotton dress and short linen jacket, accessorised with a large brimmed hat featuring a fine net veil. The boys both wore linen suits, black bow ties and white shirts which provided a welcome relief from the sea of blackness.

Mrs Sakalis and her daughter Chloe followed closely behind. They had both dressed in stunningly beautiful black tailored trouser suits made from vicuña wool which oozed utter quality and class. A fabric so rare because the animals could only be shorn every two or three years of course. Mrs Sakalis wore a more modern cloche type hat and Chloe a simple fascinator on a spray of ultra fine tulle netting.

Thalia Pantazis and the two boys stood next to the casket while the Presbyter sprinkled it with holy water. All around them the church was heavily laden with incense candles.

The service went on for at least an hour with hymn singing, psalms and eulogies commemorating Dimitris' life. It seemed he was well loved by almost everyone who knew him; giving needy people money and supporting local charities and organisations.

Lastly the most memorable of the day's readings was the one by young Chloe:

"Stop all the clocks, cut off the telephone
Prevent the dog from barking with a juicy bone
Silence the pianos and with muffled drum

Bring out the coffin, let the mourners come ..."

Not a soul moved, the silence was deafening as she continued ...

"I have read this today because it holds such fond memories of a very dear man to both my mother and I, also to Thalia and the twins. We were all at ours sharing a meal and an evening in. The rain was absolutely lashing down outside as it so often does, so we decided to watch a rerun of an old film, 'Four Weddings and a Funeral' with a few bottles of white wine.

We all loved the film. We laughed a lot but then we also all cried a lot at one point too.

It was when the actor John Hannah delivered that moving poem as a eulogy at his lover's funeral in his captivating Scottish lilt. It was of course W.H. Auden's poem, 'Funeral Blues' or 'Stop all the Clocks' as it is also known. We all agreed it was simply beautiful so to me it was the obvious tribute I could give to a very dear man today. Thank you."

Harry looked over at Andrew whose eyes were welling up, as were Yiannis Galanis's. He then dabbed his own tears with a neatly folded white handkerchief from his breast pocket, hoping the others hadn't noticed.

At this point the congregation filed outside to the rear of the church for the internment.

"Thank you all very much for attending the funeral of the much loved Dimitris Pantazis today. The family have asked me to invite you all back to The Olive Tree restaurant for Meze and drinks of Commandaria," closed the Presbyter eventually.

"I think you should go alone gentlemen for a talk with the two ladies and to ask if we could arrange a meeting for tomorrow. Let me know when you are done and I will send a car to take you back to the Holiday Inn," whispered Galanis.

"Fine," replied Andrew, "I would also like to talk to Chloe and the twins."

It was a ten minute walk to The Olive Tree with everyone chattering amicably en route. Thalia Pantazis and Angie Sakalis led the way and they soon came upon a very large olive tree just off the pavement on the grass verge. The manager and staff of the very aptly named restaurant just a few meters away greeted the party with generous glasses of Commandaria.

"Could I possibly have a Coke please?" Andrew asked. "Kanena provlima Sir. No problem."

During the Meze the noise inside crescendoed, everyone needing to talk at once as well as over each other - only louder, it seemed. Anyone passing by would have been forgiven for thinking one almighty old ding dong was going on in there.

"My ears are bleeding Andrew! I'm going to try to get Thalia Pantazis and Angie Sakalis out here to hopefully arrange a meeting with them tomorrow. You talk to the two boys and Chloe, just a friendly little chitchat and see what transpires."

Harry managed to ask both ladies to step out into the garden. They were both obviously still very emotional as Harry ordered a bottle of Ayioklima white wine from the Constantinou winery. Both ladies congratulated him on his choice which happened to be their favourite.

He smiled graciously as he poured out two large glasses, deciding not to let on he had spotted a few bottles in the cocktail cabinet at Angie Sakalis's villa.

As they relaxed a little more Harry offered his heart felt condolences. "It must have been such a terrible shock to you both," he acknowledged. He then showed Thalia Pantazis his ID card and explained to her his reason for being in Cyprus.

"Thank you Mr Webb, but Angie did phone me after you left her so I do fully understand, thank you again though. We have so much to sort out now as you will appreciate."

"I'm pleased you're fully in the picture Mrs Pantazis. Would it be possible do you think for all of us to get together for a meeting tomorrow? Yourselves of course, the twins and Chloe? Police Chief Yiannis Galanis would also like to be present."

They both consulted each other with a questioning glance then nodded their approval.

Thalia Pantazis suggested the meeting take place at a new luxury block of apartments she recently acquired in Sandy Bay, Larnaca, called 'St. Lazarus'.

"That's fine with me Thalia," agreed Angie Sakalis, "Shall we say around 10.30am?"

Again, everyone nodded in agreement.

"Good. I will give you all my new mobile number and the postcode which is 6011. We will meet up in the reception for coffee. Obviously we both need to know a lot more of exactly what happened in England and why Dimitris was shot on the beach.

Angie told me you enquired after Nico Castellanos who transgressed into a very nasty man indeed. He took us all in as we thought he was a good business partner who could be trusted. But oh no! He was trying to blackmail Dimitris. We now know we should never have trusted him. Have you any idea where he is Sir?"

"Well, all we know for sure at the moment is he caught a plane to Turkey a few days ago."

"Let's hope he stays there," the ladies replied in unison.

After saying his farewells, Harry went to find Andrew, who was still deep in conversation with the twins and Chloe.

"Sorry for interrupting but I'm just going to ring Chief Galanis for our car back to the hotel Andrew. We will see you all tomorrow," he nodded over at the youngsters.

"That's good," said Andrew, smiling at Chloe, realising Harry must have successfully arranged the meeting.

"Yes, that's lovely," Chloe smiled back at Andrew, not taking her gaze off him. "Bye for now then."

"Bye."

"Bye."

"Bye."

While they were outside Harry asked Andrew if he had learnt anything at all from the twins.

"All most interesting Harry. They are 23 years old. The slightly taller is Georgios who is training to be an airline pilot with Cyprus Airlines.

He really enjoys flying and wants to progress to the larger jets when he has a full licence. He is extremely easy to talk to and happy go lucky, probably taking after his dad in that respect.

The slightly shorter one, that's the only way I could differentiate, looks-wise at least, is Xanda. He is studying law while working with a large firm of solicitors in Nicosia. They have offices in London and the USA, New York to be precise. He aims to work in New York when he has passed his exams and is fully qualified. He is more serious and much harder to hold a conversation with than his brother.

They both enjoy football and support Nicosia. They knew a lot about our Premier League, so I managed to get a plug in about how good Newcastle are! I have both their mobile numbers."

"That's great Andrew. I have the ladies' numbers too so we can exchange later," Harry suggested.

"Ah, here's our car, let's go. I will phone Galanis on the way to brief him on the meeting tomorrow at Larnaca. He definitely wants to join us."

"I think when our guards arrive we should just settle for a bar snack Harry. I don't know about you but I am fit to burst having eaten so much Meze. It was too delicious by far!"

"I second that Andrew!"

Harry received a call at breakfast from Chief Galanis. He had arranged for them to be picked up at nine to go on to Larnaca. Their lift was spot on time and they stopped at the police station to pick up Yiannis Galanis.

On the journey the men discussed how the meeting should best be conducted. The consensus was it should remain formal with written copies given to all those in attendance. Harry agreed to take the chair but requested someone else should take down the minutes.

It took just over an hour to reach their destination, quicker than expected so they found they had time to have a look round the complex.

"What do you think it would cost to live here Harry?" asked Andrew, transfixed by the sheer opulence of the buildings and grounds surrounding him.

"Much more than the likes of you or I could possibly afford Andrew so dream on, just dream on."

Just before 10.30 everyone had arrived so they made their way to the coffee lounge. Thalia ordered the Americanos and the iced Cokes for Andrew and the boys.

"Right everyone. Thank you all for coming with special thanks to Thalia for providing us with such a beautiful venue. Chief Galanis here has asked me to take the chair for this meeting but would anyone else like to volunteer to take the minutes please?"

"I would be happy to," Chloe volunteered.

"Thank you Chloe," smiled Chief Galanis.

Harry opened proceedings by asking, "Has a solicitor been appointed to carry out any requests by Dimitris Pantazis regarding a will and carrying on with or dissolving the diamond business?"

"Yes," Thalia announced. "Angie and I have both agreed to appoint Mr Leander Prodhromos. He is the general manager of Stanvros Law. They specialise in probate and the administration of closure of businesses and estates in Cyprus. They are a well recognised international firm and have offices in London. Xanda is currently studying law in the Nicosia office."

"That sounds in order Thalia if you are both in agreement. Now, are you both aware Dimitris has a safe deposit box in the Nicosia bank?"

"Yes," answered Thalia. "We both know this but we checked with Mr Kokkinides the manager who explained he does not have knowledge of the code required to open the box so we cannot go to the bank until we are able to trace the code number. We have no idea what it could be or indeed what is inside."

"Your information is absolutely correct," replied Harry, "but I must inform you both that Andrew and I, accompanied by Chief Galanis here were all inside the vault yesterday. After three attempts I did manage to get it open."

"How on earth did you work out the code?" asked Thalia in utter amazement, "and what was in the safe?"

"Well, actually it took me sometime to come up with possible combinations but I eventually found the right one and the safe was full of small bags of diamonds."

Harry looked towards Chief Galanis, "Is it in order now Sir for me to give the safety deposit box's code?"

"Of course Harry. The ladies will need it to retrieve the diamonds as part of the Company's sale."

"Next I have to inform you of the diamonds we hold in our safe at Brighton Police Station."

Both families sat open mouthed in amazement at this latest revelation as Harry continued ...

"We have two small bags of diamonds; a case containing €30,000; a Rolex watch and Mr Pantazis's Louis Vuitton suitcase containing expensive designer clothing."

Angie looked over at Thalia, "I will be going to London soon with Chloe, staying with her in her London apartment before she recommences at the Metropolitan Police Station to continue her case revues.

I could get the train to Brighton, collect the diamonds, euros etc and decide what to do with the clothing."

"That sounds an ideal opportunity Mrs Sakalis but I wouldn't advise you travelling alone with them. Two people, Dimitris being one, have already been murdered for these."

At this point Georgios joined the conversation. "I am going to take a course of flying large planes at Heathrow airport soon. I would be pleased to accompany Angie to collect my father's belongings."

"Excellent Georgios," exclaimed his mother.

"Okay, so far so good, we're getting sorted," Harry summed up.

"Next, Chief Galanis here has his officers searching the area around Troodos for the two murder suspects, Yirgos Papadopoulos and Andreas Athanasiou. We know they were the two thugs who abducted Andrew the night we arrived in Nicosia. They were also the two who shot dead Dimitris Pantazis on Brighton beach.

They were also the two who beat up Winnie Williams in her apartment, whose beating was so violent by these men it put her in a coma from which sadly she never recovered and consequently died in Brighton hospital.

These two thugs also shot Mr Max Grey in his Classic Cars garage. Fortunately he survived and is now slowly recovering at home.

Now, we believe they were also the two who Mrs Sakalis and Chloe here are convinced forced Mr Sakalis over the edge of the cliff on the Troodos road.

They are animals with absolutely no respect for human life. I am certain they are working with Mr Nico Castellanos, who is now seeking refuge in Turkey."

"Just a recap please Mr Webb. Who was the lady Winnie Williams?" asked Angie Sakalis.

"Oh yes. She is who we call the 'bag lady'. She would walk along Brighton beach most days asking for money to buy a coffee. On the morning Dimitris was shot she had asked him if he had any spare coins. He was extremely generous and emptied his pockets of all his loose change for her. He made her day."

"Oh yes! I know of her," exclaimed Angie. "I have given her my loose change when she was walking along by the pier.

She was incredibly scruffy, wearing dirty old clothes and carrying a large threadbare bag. She was quite pleasant to talk to though and always wore a smile. So that's interesting Dimitris emptied his pockets for her."

Harry was just about to wind up the meeting when Chief Galanis's phone rang. He excused himself saying he would take the call outside. Within a minute he rushed back in and beckoned urgently to Harry and Andrew.

"Come quickly! My men have located the old farm where the two men are hiding!"

Harry and Andrew jumped up, said their goodbyes and rushed out.

"Please take care Andrew!" Chloe called after them ...

Chapter 13

Kites rise highest against the wind, not with it

The police car screeched up outside and they piled in. Chief Galanis instructed the driver to engage the blue lights and to drive as quickly as he dared ...

Then he rang his office ordering a four wheel drive Range Rover be made available for them immediately - equipped with three extra guns, ammunition and first aid kits.

"... I will also need a second Range Rover with four police officers ready to follow us!

... and a megaphone."

The driver careered along at breakneck speed and they arrived at the police station within 45 minutes. The hair raising experience had knocked fifteen minutes off their earlier journey.

As he screeched to a halt they all jumped out. The two Range Rovers were already waiting for them, including in the second the two police officers complete with all the extras Galanis had demanded.

"Okay, foot down!" he instructed their driver. "Blue lights engaged until we are out of Nicosia then keep them off!"

The road was rough and hazardous in parts.

"Right, we want to get there safely," Galanis instructed the driver, "... so, fast but safe! I anticipate we should be there in one and a half hours."

On the way they discussed means of extracting the two thugs from the farmhouse. They decided on surrounding the building, cutting off various avenues of escape, though this would only be possible to determine exactly of course when they saw the layout of the outbuildings on their arrival.

"If not then it will be a case of trust your instincts. I have every faith in you both my friends. We know it will not be easy," Galanis smiled back at Harry and Andrew.

"Kites rise highest against the wind, not with it," he encouraged them.

Andrew looked at him, awaiting confirmation of whose quote it was ... he didn't have to wait long.

"Winston Churchill, an incredible man and an absolute master of stoicism. In a conflict who better to take inspiration from, eh?

We must remember his example, 'Do not look for comfort. Do not resent challenges,' and you two won't. You will excel. We will win against these scumbags today no matter what they throw at us gentlemen, of that I am most sure."

Andrew was convinced it would be the farmhouse they held him captive and pumped up by Galanis's pep talk he offered as much information as he could recall. If there was to be a confrontation he was all set to take the lead. He was the youngest and the fittest as well as having a personal score to settle ... he had a shed load of stored up adrenaline pumping, pumping, pumping through his young body.

"If it is the same place, there wasn't very much space at the rear, just a path into the woods I believe. I remember there were also some ramshackle outbuildings to the side."

They were making good time along the Troodos road so at one point Galanis asked his driver to take his foot off the pedal along the next series of sharp bends.

"This is where Dimitris Pantazis was run off the road," he explained. Sure enough just around the next hairpin bend was the damaged safety barrier, serving as a grim reminder.

"I will get authorisation for this barrier to be changed for a much larger one on our return."

"It certainly needs a replacement Sir," agreed the driver. "Should have been sorted out well before now."

"How are we doing for time driver?" asked Galanis, his mind fully refocused once more on the perilous task ahead.

"Okay Sir, according to the sat-nav we are thirty minutes away now."

"Just watch the side lanes when we turn off the main Troodos road. I'm looking on the map. It's very near the UN green line buffer zone at Skoumoassa, a thickly wooded area five or six miles from the RAF radar units.

I have asked our station to send up two ambulances as a precautionary measure and have just received confirmation they have both been deployed and are on their way."

Andrew was looking over Chief Galanis's shoulder at the map in his lap. He was absolutely certain now they were heading straight to where the two men had held him captive.

"Nearly there Sir, just a couple more bends," advised the driver.

Andrew was now pulling at the leash ... he absolutely needed retribution not just for his suffering at the thugs' hands but for that of Winnie, Dimitris and Chloe's father.

"Here we are Sir! See, there's our police car parked under those trees to the left," he pointed, "and our officers are standing by. Our second car is just pulling in behind us now."

They jumped out of their respective vehicles. Galanis called them all together.

"Listen, this is what we do: Driver, stay by the two police cars and maintain radio contact."

He then introduced Harry and Andrew to the others, as 'the two detectives from England who are wearing bullet proof vests'.

"Right, when we inch closer I want you all to spread out and access the rear and sides of the main farmhouse.

Pigaine – arga, go slowly!

Be extremely vigilant and careful. These two men have already murdered two innocent people in England and one man over here in Cyprus. They will not hesitate to kill again. They have guns."

Galanis held up the binoculars through which he could clearly see the two men by the farmhouse door.

"One has long tzintzer, ginger hair."

"That's them Sir," Andrew confirmed. "The other is smaller in stature."

"Confirmed. I have him in my sights now. I can also confirm they are both wearing guns."

As prearranged they all panned out and stealthily edged towards the farmhouse.

When they were pretty close Chief Galanis engaged the megaphone.

"Stamata! Stop! Stay where you are! Lay your guns on the ground and put your hands on your heads! You are completely surrounded. I repeat you are completely surrounded."

The thugs reacted by firing three random shots towards Galanis, then ran inside the farmhouse, slamming the door behind them.

Galanis called out again louder, *"Come out with your hands on your heads. This will be your final warning."*

After a few minutes the door opened. One of them came out wielding a gun. He took aim and fired a few shots at the police officers then sharply swung around facing Andrew.

Andrew could see the whites of his eyes as two shots were fired towards him, he ducked as one bullet buzzed over his shoulder while the second hit the ground by his feet.

Using his combat training Andrew deftly dived to the ground while simultaneously firing two brilliantly aimed shots, both hitting the gunman in the chest. He slumped lifeless to the ground just to the right of the door.

The second gunman then appeared at the doorway firing three shots towards the other police officer, Chief Galanis and Harry.

The first shot did hit the officer in the thigh. He yelped in agony as he hit the ground. The second bullet hit the rocks close to Galanis which caused it to ricochet sharply, hitting Harry in the chest.

The impact brought him heavily to the ground. He fell back with considerable force and cracked his head open on a giant boulder. Blood gushed heavily from the wound.

The third shot shaved Galanis's head. Galanis responded with two perfect aims; the first hitting the gunman in the heart; the second piercing straight through his neck and splitting open his carotid artery. The result was bloody. Very bloody!

Andrew immediately ran over to help Harry. He lay lifeless with a stream of blood gushing from the back of his head. The police Range Rover quickly appeared with the first aid kits and Andrew was able to apply a large swab with pressure to Harry's injury to try to hopefully stem the bleeding until the ambulances arrived.

The remaining police officers kicked the back door of the farmhouse in, then swarmed through the building, ensuring it was completely empty. It was.

They walked over to the two motionless gunmen, checking their pulses. There weren't any. They both lay dead.

"Well, aren't we all exceptionally good kite flyers!" announced Galanis with a modicum of pride.

Chapter 14

Both optimists and pessimists contribute to society ...
The optimist invents the aeroplane, the pessimist the parachute

... but it wasn't over yet. Chief Galanis ordered his men to find blankets to cover the two dead men.

Meanwhile slightly further afield Andrew was concerned for Harry. He had regained consciousness to a certain extent but his eyes, though now wide open, were totally void of emotion. He was distant, not knowing where he was.

Andrew tried over and over again to engage him in conversation, whilst willing the ambulances to arrive soon. "Please come soon! Please!"

Harry remained 'distant' as the blood continued to ooze heavily through the wadding, forcing Andrew to dutifully wrap layers more bandages around his head from the first aid kits, forming a gigantic turban.

"... Please, please come soon! Where on earth are you?" he silently pleaded.

"Stay awake Harry! Keep your eyes open! OPEN!"

He tore off Harry's bullet proof vest - the bullet was still lodged inside it. "Good job you were wearing this vest Harry, looks like the bullet was on target for your heart. It saved your life! ... You will have a nasty bruise on your chest though ..."

Meanwhile Chief Galanis and another officer were treating their man who was shot in the thigh. He too was bleeding profusely. He had a nasty deep, open wound exposing much flesh and more worryingly his femur bone.

The officer was yelling out in obvious agony.

"Where the hell are those ambulances?" yelled Galanis. "This man is in a very bad way and in acute pain."

Another officer ran up clenching a single dose of morphine but there was no more in the first aid kit.

"I've just received a call Sir, informing us the ambulances will be at least another 45 minutes yet. They encountered a very nasty road traffic accident en route and are dealing with many casualties on the roadside."

"What! WHAT!! W H A T !!!" Galanis hollered.

At this point Andrew intervened, shouting over, "Sir, we could call the RAF Radar Unit and ask Alan Groves if we could take Harry and your officer, sorry, I don't know his name, there. When they took me in I went to a small hospital unit there used for local emergencies."

"Oh! Yes Andrew, that's an excellent idea. His name by the way is Xephyr Samparas."

Galanis rang Groves ...

"Yes, come right away I will have our doctor ready for you."

"Right Andrew. You travel with Harry and Xephyr in the police vehicle. I will wait until an ambulance arrives to take these two dead men, Yirgos Papadopoulos and Andreas Athanasiou to the police morgue.

Give me a call when you get there and I will alert the American hospital along the Paphos road. I know the doctors there, I've used them before. They will remove the bullet from Xephyr's thigh and give Harry a head and chest X-ray. They will probably both be in hospital for a while.

Let's hope they don't deteriorate. This time delay in getting them treatment could prove crucial!"

Andrew tried talking to Harry once again but 'no answer' boomed the loud reply! Though his eyes were completely vacant at least they were open ... he consoled himself with that thought but wasn't sure it was relevant.

"Harry, Harry, please stay awake. Did you hear me earlier? Your bullet proof vest saved your life. Isn't that good?"

"Ummm," Harry mumbled.

"That's great Harry, do you remember what has just happened?"

Harry tried mumbling but no more sounds came out.

The police driver drove carefully and within minutes they arrived safely at the RAF unit. The doctor was there to meet them and helped the two patients onto beds. He attended Harry first as Xephyr's earlier dose of morphine seemed to be helping him somewhat.

He congratulated Andrew on his emergency bandaging skills.

"This could take a while to heal," he advised Andrew. I am concerned he lost consciousness and is woozy so an X-ray and CT scan will definitely be carried out at the main hospital. If there is a contusion on the brain itself, a blood clot or swelling inside the brain around that area could occur. That would have serious ramifications I'm afraid."

"So what would happen if it is the case doctor?"

"Looking on the pessimistic side surgery would be performed to remove the hematoma that is compressing the brain or raising the pressure inside the skull. They will be able to assess this more precisely at the hospital though. I assure you every precaution will be taken to look after his welfare. You must remain optimistic at this moment in time. It would be great if he starts talking to us."

The doctor moved on to Xephyr's bed. He carefully bathed the gaping bullet wound on the officer's leg; covered it with a sterile dressing pad and gave him another morphine injection.

"There, that should last him until he arrives at the hospital."

Looking concerned the doctor then took Xephyr's temperature.

"Is everything okay doctor?" asked Andrew.

"Well once again, best to be optimistic. The very good news is the bullet somehow missed the femoral artery which is vulnerable as it lies superficially so consequently is unprotected by any muscle or bone."

"... and the bad news?"

"He has a temperature so again, looking on the cautious side the hospital will probably opt to give him antibiotics. As it is a large open wound he has here it could easily have become infected especially as he was lying in a filthy old junk filled yard for such a long period of time.

They would not want sepsis to occur so will conduct the appropriate tests for that immediately. Sepsis does respond well to antibiotics though - if they are administered promptly.

Well done on thinking of getting these men to us young man - you could well have saved their lives by doing so!"

At this juncture Andrew rang Chief Galanis. He explained the two patients had been examined by the RAF duty doctor who was referring them both to the American hospital for further tests and treatment.

He explained the doctor's overriding instincts were to remain optimistic though there could well be a few problems on the horizon.

He then went in to see Harry, whose eyes were now wide open and he seemed to be a little more responsive.

"How are you now?" he smiled. "I have been really worried about you, you know. That was a nasty fall and you took the full impact on the back of your head. You lost so much blood Harry."

"I f-f-f-e-l-t a bit v o o z y A ndr e w, but I'mmm m u c h b - etta nowww."

"Oh great! You're beginning to talk again Harry, but they will be sending you for an X-ray and a CT scan to the American hospital to make doubly sure there is no serious damage."

The ambulance arrived and the doctor helped the paramedics get both patients aboard and ready for the transfer to the American hospital. He informed the crew of the treatments already administered including the two morphine injections Xephyr had been given and of his temperature. Also of Harry's loss of consciousness and total incoherence at the scene and his wooziness now, suggesting a CT scan on his arrival at the hospital.

Andrew asked if it would be okay to travel with them.

"Of course, no problem Sir. The Chief asked us to take you along and for the driver to return to the farm to collect him."

It took two hours to get to the hospital at Nicosia. Two nurses and a doctor met the ambulance at the entrance.

"We will take Mr Harry Webb straight to X-ray then on for a CT scan. We were told he fell heavily backwards and took the full force of the impact to the back of his head. Nasty!

The officer Samparas we will take straight on down to the operating theatre to remove the bullet from his thigh. We will also be starting him on strong antibiotics immediately.

My name is Ally Martizez. I will make sure both gentlemen get the best treatment available and hopefully they should soon make a full recovery.

Chief Galanis told me you are two detectives from Brighton, England and are investigating two murders."

"Yes Doctor Martizez, that's correct."

"Please, just call me Ally."

Officer Xephyr Samparas was soon taken down to theatre and Harry was just being wheeled to the X-ray department when he called over to Andrew, slightly more articulate now, "Pees phone the Dee-Zee-S. Ave you izz numb-ba?"

"Yes, I have his number Harry and I will update him on the day's events and will hopefully get to him before he hears it all over the radio and TV. I will give Mrs Pantazis and Mrs Sakalis an update too."

'G o o d. Ohh, and Sh e a f Galla - - too. I ope t'be out of ear z o o n."

"Okay Harry."

"No. You definitely will not be out of here soon Mr Webb!" doctor Ally butted in. Best possible scenario you will be here for two to three nights!"

Andrew could not quite make out what Harry was mumbling as he was wheeled away ...

"I believe you are staying at the Holiday Inn Andrew?"

"That's correct Ally."

"Just wait in Reception a moment. One of my staff lives near there, he can give you a lift back."

Andrew made a call to Angie Sakalis and Thalia Pantazis while he was waiting. He also rang Chief Galanis who was still at the farm.

"So, do you know if we should be optimistic or pessimistic at the moment Andrew?"

"Just a bit too early to say Sir."

"Well, as the saying goes, 'Both optimists and pessimists contribute to society. The optimist invents the aeroplane, the pessimist the parachute.'"

Andrew waited for Galanis to explain where the saying originated. How did the man do it? He was a walking reference book on all things ever written in literature.

"George Bernard Shaw of course. A great wit ... Anyway, be ready at 9.30 in the morning and I will drive you on to see how our two patients are. Then in the afternoon we have to

181

return to the bank. The ladies need to open the safe deposit box again so the manager requests we are present.

And of course we have statements to fill out with a full report of today's events. When you have completed yours I will get it translated into Greek. I have Harry's gun and bullet proof vest here to return to the armoury. I think that's it."

A young man came into reception, "Hello, Mr Andrew?"

"Yes."

"I am a junior doctor. I have just finished my shift and understand you would like a lift to the Holiday Inn?"

"Thank you so much," smiled Andrew, following him to his car.

Andrew was soon back in his room absolutely shattered after the day's events. He turned on the tv. As he had walked through Reception towards the lifts just a minute ago the news channel was showing the day's events on the big screen so he had rushed up to listen to it in English on the BBC World News Channel.

They reported it quite accurately he thought. 'Two Cypriot men were shot dead at a disused farm near the Green Line buffer zone at Skoumoassa. One was shot by an English detective, the other by Police Chief Yiannis Galanis.

Both men fired the first shots at the police officers, one of whom received a bullet to his thigh and the English detective was shot in the chest.

The two injured officers were rushed to the nearby RAF Radar Station then transferred to the American Hospital in Nicosia. No further news was yet available.'

It was weird hearing about their exploits on the television. He placed an order for burger and chips to be brought to his room, where he continued to make more calls.

The first was to DCS John Street. It was 11pm in the UK so Andrew apologised for the lateness of the call.

The DCS was relieved Andrew was okay, but worried for Harry. He had seen and heard the day's accounts on the late evening news but they hadn't named the English detective who was shot in the chest.

"Yes, he was Sir but thankfully he was wearing a bullet proof vest. The problem was the impact threw him violently backwards and he received a nasty wound to the back of his head. They were about to do X-rays and scans on him when I left the hospital."

"Okay Andrew. Thanks for keeping me informed and for sending the daily reports to Angela. What are you doing tomorrow?"

"Chief Galanis is calling for me at 9.30am and we are going on to the American hospital to see how they both are. We are then making our way to the Nicosia Bank. The ladies want to open the safe deposit box again and Mr Kokkinides, the manager, wants us to be present also. I don't know why, perhaps it's a bank regulation.

I just hope I will not be shut inside there for too long though as I become quite claustrophobic."

"Sorry to hear that Andrew but remember the best antidote for that is deep breaths in and even longer breaths out. I understand it slows the heart rate down.

I still can't quite figure out you know how Harry worked out that combination."

"Well, that's Harry isn't it? There is not a single lock that foxes him for long!"

"No. Well don't forget to phone home tomorrow Andrew as your family will certainly see reports on the television or in the newspapers."

"Yes Sir. I do plan to call them early."

"Will you phone me from the hospital? I will phone Liz, though knowing Harry he is speaking to her right now. Please give him our best wishes for a speedy recovery and ask him to phone me if he can."

"I will Sir, but he will not be phoning anyone tonight. He is not well enough."

"Oh??" questioned the DCS concerned.

"But the doctor did say to remain optimistic though Sir," Andrew quickly reassured him. "These things take time."

"Okay ... well Andrew I hope you get a good restful night."

"Thank you Sir, kalinychta."

"And kalinychta to you Andrew ... pleased your Greek is coming along nicely."

Andrew had a pretty restless sleep. He was worried and deeply concerned about Harry's head injury.

He took an early shower before breakfast and turned on the TV. Every channel he flicked through was reporting news of the shootings: the BBC; the USA CBS Station from Detroit; the local stations, everyone, everywhere ...

Down in the restaurant while he was taking breakfast guests were looking over at him and whispering hands over mouths. It felt so strange not having Harry with him or a police guard nearby.

One couple came over to him and enthused, "Well done son! We won't ask you any questions but we saw the news this morning and guessed it was you. We hope your colleague will be okay. You take care now," they added with a smile as they left the restaurant.

No sooner had they left when a large man wearing an oversized straw hat, a white tee shirt covered in huge red flowers, red shorts and canvas shoes dropped himself into a seat at his table. He just sat eyeballing him for a minute. Andrew drew his chair back a few inches.

"Hi fella!" he suddenly hollered in a broad American accent. "I'm Guy Anderson from the CBS, Chicago. We would like an exclusive on the shooting yesterday. We would pay ya a thousand dollars!"

Andrew was flabbergasted. How did this unsavoury man know he was involved?

"I'm sorry Sir," Andrew answered him politely, "but it's against our police regulations to give any information out to anyone on a case under investigation."

Just then he noticed a police car stop outside. "Sorry Sir, I have to go now."

"Well, I bet ya they'd go higher son!"

Andrew made a hasty retreat.

Chief Galanis was sat in the front as usual and asked Andrew if he was okay.

"Kalimera. Yes thank you Sir. I have just had a reporter from the USA News Channel wanting me to give him an exclusive story for a payment of $1,000!"

"Well, I hope you didn't accept it. It's a dismissal case in Cyprus you know as well as in England."

"No Sir, I don't intend to of course. He hinted they would pay me more but even if they offered me ten thousand I obviously still would not accept. He was very uncouth!

How was it at the farm Sir, after we left?"

"It took a while to get cleared up Andrew and for the ambulance to eventually take away the two bodies.

There was also a slight complication. As the farm was on the green line buffer zone the Turkish police came along and became embroiled in the whole situation.

They wanted to take the two bodies away with them but there was no way I could allow that to happen, so we ended up loading them both on our ambulance, quite unceremoniously and driving away at speed!

The two of them are now in our Nicosia morgue. It is my duty to contact their families unfortunately. I'm expecting trouble on that front but it's all part of the job I suppose.

When we return to the station after visiting the bank, I will call your DCS John Street. I have a few things to sort out with him and depending on how Harry is ascertain when we can get you both back on a flight to Gatwick."

"Yes Sir, I did tell him I would call him from the hospital too."

The driver drew up at the front of the American Hospital and as they walked through to the reception doctor Ally Martizez came through one of the side doors.

"Good morning gentlemen. If you will both follow me to my office I can update you before I take you to the wards. Please take a seat."

He looked quite concerned Andrew thought, which worried him somewhat ...

"Well the position with Harry Webb is this. We took a CT scan of his head. There were signs of a mild bleed around his brain but his cognitive responses are now good.

He also suffered from severe concussion but is now fully aware, able to speak without slurring his words and is most responsive. I think, however, another day or two before he should fly home would be advisable - but the man, well, he is very stubborn is he not?"

Andrew breathed a deep sigh of relief. It sounded as though Harry was 'Harry' once again!

"He lost a lot of blood. We have stapled the wound on his head as staples are more secure than stitches. He will need to keep his head bandaged for another four or five days.

With regard to his chest. It is going to be extremely painful for a few weeks. It very much looks as though this has happened to him before. Do you know anything about that Andrew?"

"He hasn't mentioned it Ally but I will certainly ask him when I get the opportunity."

"Okay, well as I said he is very headstrong. I want to keep him in at least another 24 hours - he wants to leave today so see what you think when you visit him. I am as they say leaving the ball in your court."

As Chief Galanis didn't respond to this phrase Andrew assumed it was of no literary consequence.

"Now, with regard to your Officer Xephyr Samparas Chief Galanis. We had problems removing the bullet from his thigh. It was deeply embedded and the entry wound was extremely close to the femoral artery.

The wound was filthy and we feared sepsis might occur. We did treat him for this immediately as a precaution. His temperature was high, he was breathless, faint and nauseous - he was displaying all the signs in other words.

Unfortunately, despite our prompt reactions we could not catch it soon enough because of course he lay in that dirty yard for so long. With a deep, gaping wound that is catastrophic.

We have managed to curb the infection however, so we are at present hopeful we can save his leg from amputation.

He is not as confused as he was after his operation last night and has managed to speak to his wife this morning. She is coming in to visit him this afternoon."

"I'm so sorry to hear he has been suffering," said Chief Galanis. "I will call his wife later."

They all gathered their thoughts.

"Okay, you guys, let's go up to the wards."

Chief Galanis headed straight for Xephyr's room while Andrew made a beeline to Harry's.

Harry was sat in bed smiling. His head bandage looked even larger than ever, a bit like Roger Hargreaves's Mr Bump! "Hello Andrew, I'm so pleased to see you. I'm hoping to get out of here today, please help me."

"Well Harry, the doctor wants you to stay in for one more night, though two would have been preferable. You've got a worrying head wound there as well as taking a sizeable impact to your chest from that bullet. Has this happened to you before by any chance?"

"Yes, twice!" he grinned.

"Well Harry let's hope that was the last time!"

"Oh, don't keep talking about me, I'm okay. But WOW! Andrew. Didn't you and Chief Galanis have some brilliant shots out there? You were both magnificent!"

"Yes Harry but am I so glad I did that combat training course and passed my shooting exam at Hendon Police College!"

"You should be proud Andrew. Very proud!" Harry praised again. "Do you know what happened to my gun?"

"Galanis has it along with your bullet infested vest!"

"Oh that's good! As long as it's in safe hands."

"I gave my gun and vest to the police driver to take back with him. I'm so relieved I don't have to wear it here again.

"Have you spoken with Liz Harry?"

"Yes. The DCS kindly rang her first and I spoke to her just a while ago Andrew. All the reports on the BBC World News apparently reported one of the English detectives was shot in the chest. She was beside herself!"

"That's right. Not just the BBC but all over the USA and as far afield as Timbuktu I wouldn't be surprised! We are plastered all over the world newspapers too."

Harry turned more somber. "Liz wants me to talk to the DCS about taking an early retirement Andrew. I suppose I could do but it's something I have never had reason to consider in the past.

I'm fifty eight now and could in theory have retired at fifty five but I decided to carry on, mainly to get the extra pension, but perhaps I should weigh up my options again."

"Well Harry, wait until your head is clearer then have a quiet conversation with John Street. See what he thinks."

"Yes, I will," he agreed.

"I had a call from him just before you arrived. He wanted to know how I was of course, but was also full of praise for you Andrew! He was very pleased with the way you handled the shooting at the farm."

Andrew was touched.

"He also said you are going with Chief Galanis to the bank later this morning with Thalia Pantazis and Angie Sakalis. They want to open the safe deposit box again apparently?"

"Yes, that's right. It was so lucky for them you were able to work out the combination. Sheer genius that!"

Just then Chief Galanis burst in, "Harry! How are you dear man?"

"Much better now, thank you Sir. The bullet proof vest worked a treat. How is your officer Sir?"

"He isn't good Harry, I'm afraid. The bullet penetrated deep into his thigh, as did some dirt and they had to cut deeply to get the darned thing out. The delay in getting him here allowed sepsis to take a hold. That blessed yard was so filthy and the ambulances didn't show ... well, anyway, he is on strong antibiotics so hopefully they can save his leg ...

It will be a waiting game though."

"I'm so sorry to hear that Sir."

"I've had a word with the doctors about you Harry. You must stay another night in hospital - and no arguments please! You can't fly for another few days anyway with that head injury! They need to give you a thorough check before you leave - especially after all that drivel you were spouting off yesterday!"

Harry looked questioningly over to Andrew.

Andrew nodded his head. "Yes, you were Harry."

"Yes you most certainly were!" concurred Galanis. "Surely you can see sense now man?"

Harry mumbled something incoherent under his breath ... "Ur, what's that Harry, are you with us?"

"Yes Sir."

"Great. So I require young Andrew at the bank with me today. We have been asked to accompany the ladies to take their diamonds to their Solicitors, Stanvros Law for a meeting with a Mr Prodhromos. He requires us to be witnesses to their signatures. He is selling their diamond business for them as you know along with all the stock so will keep the gems in his safe.

The deal cannot be finalised of course until Thalia Pantazis has collected the diamonds you hold at your Brighton police station.

When you next speak to your DCS Street could you update him please?"

"Yes Sir, I will."

"I have promised to phone him too Harry, so please confirm I will call him later."

"No problem Andrew."

"Okay, young Andrew let's go. We have much to do today and still haven't submitted our reports," ordered Galanis, now already halfway out of the door.

"And Harry, are you up to filling out your report my man? If so either we will collect it later or perhaps you could email it to my secretary, Sophia."

"Okay Sir, I will."

When they arrived at the bank the driver dropped them off at the front door then went to park up as before.

As they waited in Reception a taxi pulled up outside. It was Mrs Pantazis and Mrs Sakalis. When she entered Angie Sakalis rushed over to Andrew and threw her arms round him.

"My dear boy, how pleased we are you are safe."

191

"Yes indeed and how is Harry?" asked Thalia Pantazis.

"He is recovering well now thank you. We were worried for the first twenty four hours as he took a heavy fall onto the back of his head but he is improving hour by hour. He is being kept in hospital for another night though, just to be on the safe side."

"Which hospital is he in?" asked Thalia.

"The American one on the Paphos Road," replied Chief Galanis.

"Oh good! That's the best one Sir. We hope your officer makes a good recovery also. We all listened intently to the CBS News and there was a report in the Cyprus Mail but it didn't mention any names."

"No I have stopped any press releases."

"We assume the two men who were shot dead were the two who pushed my husband's car over the cliff?"

"Yes, they were Mrs Sakalis and they were the two wanted for the shooting of Mr Dimitris Pantazis on Brighton beach, so my dear I would say that was divine retribution wouldn't you?"

At this juncture the bank receptionist came out and informed them Mr Kokkinides was now ready to take them to the vaults. "If you will just follow me please."

Mr Kokkinides took them down to the bowels of the building.

"Yassou, I will leave you now," he announced.

It was cold in there and Andrew hoped it wouldn't take them long.

Without wasting a second Thalia Pantazis and Angie Sakalis headed straight for their safe deposit box. They entered once again the code Harry had given them. It clicked six times then the door released.

They had brought a leather case along with them. They carefully counted out twenty eight small velvet bags, opened just a few to check them, and yes they held diamonds.

"Okay, that's empty now," declared Thalia as she put the final bag into the case.

"Could you press the door buzzer Andrew please? We can go now." She closed the door and scrambled the code.

Mr Kokkinides opened the vault within seconds, to Andrew's delight. "Everything okay?" he asked politely.

"Yes Sir," replied Mrs Pantazis, "thank you."

As they left the bank Thalia Pantazis asked if either Chief Galanis or Andrew could carry the case to the solicitor's office for them. It wasn't very far to walk but they would feel happier, more secure if one of the men could take it.

"No probs. I will," volunteered Andrew.

"Don't run off with it," joked Angie, laughing.

"He wouldn't get very far," chipped in Chief Galanis. "I'd have every police officer in Cyprus after him."

They very soon reached the offices of Stanvros Law and Mr Prodhromos welcomed everyone warmly into his personal office.

"The first thing I must do is lock your case in the company safe. If both you ladies would like to accompany me we will just check it's contents before I do so. I must also ask you both to sign a Safe Entry form, agreeing the contents.

If you gentlemen would care to take a seat here we will not be long."

Mrs Pantazis and Mrs Sakalis followed Mr Prodhromos to the safe room. They were both amazed at the high tech security required just to enter.

Mr Prodhromos emptied the contents of the leather case onto a bench then counted out both slowly and deliberately twenty eight small bags all containing diamonds.

He looked inside each bag then weighed out their contents on a set of Ohaus precision balance scales. They totalled 8.625 pounds or 3.912 kilos.

Both ladies checked and agreed the amount and the weight with Mr Prodhromos, whereupon he stacked them neatly on the top shelf of the safe then deftly entered the code.

"Right ladies, I will arrange for an independent professional valuation on these as soon as possible and will inform you of their total carat content. Is this the entire diamond stock your company owns?"

"Oh, no Sir!" replied Angie Sakalis. "There are two more bags in the safe at the Brighton police station, England. I will be collecting those in a few weeks time. I will then take them on to London's Hatton Garden where they will be sold.

I will of course request the buyer sends you a receipt of purchase. Will this be satisfactory for your records?"

"Yes, Mrs Sakalis, thank you very much. If we could now go back to my office and rejoin the gentlemen. Follow me please ..."

They went back through Reception to his office, which looked more like a palace and the forms requiring signatures for dissolving the business had been laid out already by his secretary.

All that remained now was for the solicitor to precisely confirm with them how the final monies would be distributed.

Chief Galanis and Andrew were asked to check the documents before signing and witnessing them in triplicate. Everything completed and rubber stamped they finally left the building.

"There's a coffee bar nearby if anyone is interested," suggested Angie Sakalis and very soon they were making themselves comfortable around a small table. They ordered three Cappuccinos with extra shots and an iced Coke from the smartly dressed waiter. There then followed an enthusiastic discussion on just how successful and fulfilling the day had been. Happy chatter and smiles were definitely the order of the day.

Chief Galanis thought the distribution of monies upon completion was most fair - with 35% each allocated to the two ladies, Angie and Thalia and 10% each for their offspring, Chloe, Georgios and Xanda.

"Yes, a brilliant distribution ladies!" he congratulated them, "though I did think Mr Prodhromos' fees were rather extortionate!"

"Those plush offices do have to be financed somehow Chief Galanis," Angie conjectured with a smile.

"Ummmm!"

"Yes," we did both agree his fees at the onset," concurred Thalia, "as we were both still the main directors."

"I read that Nico Castellanos's contract had been terminated nearly a year ago," Galanis added. "Has he been hassling you both for some time?"

"Yes Sir, he was bombarding us and our children with threats."

"Well, the last I heard he is being investigated by the Turkish police in Ankara. I am in contact with the Chief of Police there so will keep you all well informed of any developments on that front."

"Just changing the subject," intervened Andrew, "but if I am about when you come to London and Brighton Mrs Sakalis, I would like to meet up with yourself and Chloe."

"Of course Andrew, we would be delighted to see you again." Andrew's face lit up like a beacon.

They were just finishing their coffees when Chief Galanis's phone rang.

He had been outside about five minutes taking the call and when he reentered the room he wore the biggest of smiles.

"Well ladies, here is some brilliant news to polish off a most successful day!

That was the Chief of Police in Ankara, Chief Ahmet. He has just informed me they have arrested Nico Castellanos on charges of extortion, violent racketeering and blackmail."

"Whoopee!" came a spontaneous happy chorus.

"He will be tried in Ankara shortly and Ahmet thought a prison sentence for a minimum of 15 years will be meted out."

Another loud "Whoopee," echoed through the coffee bar.

"Let's order a brandy," suggested Thalia. "How about you two? We must celebrate this momentous news."

"Sorry ladies we are on duty but we will happily raise a coffee cup and a Coke to your Metaxas!" And they did!

"So what are your future plans, when Mr Prodhromos has finalised all your business?"

"I will keep the Villa at Antonios, Nicosia as my main residence and now I have acquired the luxury block of flats at Larnaca I find myself wanting to do the same at Polis. That's a fast growing tourist area. When Xanda has qualified as a lawyer he will go out to the New York offices so I may look to purchase some apartments there also."

"That sounds excellent and well thought out Mrs Pantazis. What about you, Mrs Sakalis?"

"Well, at present I have the villa at Amathus, the two hotels in Paphos and the apartment in Brighton, so we are both going down the property route. I might also consider buying a penthouse apartment on the London Embankment for Chloe."

"Well ladies, it sounds as though you have it all sorted. Congratulations and good luck in the future to you all."

Changing the subject, Angie Sakalis asked Andrew how long he thought he would be in Cyprus for and how Harry was progressing.

"Well, talk of the devil, I have just this minute received a text from Harry. Much to his annoyance they are insisting on keeping him in hospital overnight again but we can collect him in the morning.

He will be a bear with a sore head caged in there against his will and I'm sure they will literally throw him at us tomorrow!"

"That's good news Andrew," chipped in Chief Galanis. "I will get my secretary to book you both flights to Gatwick the following day. I will also ask her to phone your DCS John Street with the flight arrival time.

We should be getting back to the station now if we have covered everything for you two charming ladies?"

"Yes, thank you Sir and antio sas, goodbye and efcharisto," beamed Thalia Pantazis.

"And Andrew I will let you know the next time I will be in London with Chloe," smiled Angie Sakalis.

Both men left the cafe and walked back to the car. Chief Galanis's driver was waiting patiently. On the way back to the station Yiannis Galanis told Andrew they had better get their reports on file post haste.

"My secretary Sophia will look after you Andrew. It will be quicker if you sit by her, tell her exactly how you reacted to the shooting etc. she will then record what you say in both English and Greek," advised the Chief.

Chapter 15

Making less sense than the Jabberwocky my son!

"**I** *was going through my report just now when I noticed the man I shot was Yirgos Papadopoulos - the one born in England. The man you shot was Andreas Athanasiou - the one born in Cyprus. That is oh so fortunate for you Andrew!"*

"Really Sir, why is that?"

"Well, had you shot Yirgos Papadopoulos you would now have the whole of the London Cypriot mafia after you from the moment you set foot back in England!"

Andrew gulped as he turned a sickly shade of green. "Really Sir? I didn't know that. I expect Harry knows all about them though ..."

"Oh yes Andrew, your Harry is an extremely experienced and clever man. He knows all there is to know about them. He would not have wanted to alarm you though. I do believe he is the most unpretentious, kindly man I have ever had the honour of meeting."

"Yes, he is certainly my mentor. Thank you for explaining that Sir. I will ask him on the journey home."

"When we are ready Andrew I would like you to come home with me to have dinner with us. I will call my wife Katerina, if that's okay with you of course?"

"Yes Sir I would like that. It's a bit embarrassing in the hotel dining room - it feels as though everyone is looking at me."

"Fine. I will ask her to get a few Cokes in for you."

Reports all complete Galanis sighed, "Right let's go Andrew!" He had his car in the station car park and explained he lived near Laxia, just four miles away.

"Just call me Yiannis when we are off duty Andrew."

As they drove Andrew admired the scenery. "Yes we love it in this part of Cyprus, we've been here for four happy years now. Ah, here we are."

They pulled into the driveway of a very smart villa, nowhere near as large as Mrs Sakalis's but beautiful all the same. The walls were whitewashed and prettily complemented with apple green woodwork around the windows, on the door and around it's frame. Katerina met them at the door and gave Yiannis an affectation kiss and Andrew a warm hug.

"Yassou kalispera," greeted Andrew.

Katerina laughed and said, "You speak Greek Andrew?"

"Oh, no, no, no. I am just tying to pick up a few words Katerina."

Yiannis smiled. "It's a lovely evening, we will eat outside I think. I have a barbecue ready and Katerina makes an excellent Greek salad."

Andrew walked around the gardens and took a lingering look at the inviting pool. Katerina walked with him. "We are so lucky living here. The property and upkeep of the garden and pool comes with Yiannis's job."

"Very nice," replied Andrew with feeling. "I would love a job and house here one day."

"Well Andrew you just have to keep working hard and it will happen I am sure. Yiannis has kept me informed of your abduction and so soon after your arrival in Nicosia too."

"Yes, not a very pleasant welcome but thankfully I managed to escape."

"Thank God you did Andrew. Now, I can smell the barbecue is ready. I will fetch you a cold Coke."

"Thank you Katerina, I'm ready to eat now! It has been a long day."

After a most hospitable and delicious meal Yiannis asked Andrew if he was still hankering to go on a run before he returned home.

"Oh Yes! I would love to."

"Right, then tomorrow is the day young Andrew! At 7.30 sharp and I will run with you! Then after breakfast we can collect Harry. It is best for you to run with someone who knows their way round the city walls as it weaves in and out of the green buffer zone."

"That's great thank you so much, but are you fit to run?" he enquired with a smile.

"Cheeky young whippersnapper!" laughed Yiannis, "Am I fit to run indeed! Well you'll see!"

Katerina then joined in the conversation. Please don't worry about him Andrew. Yiannis ran regularly in the Athens marathon when we are living there. He is fitter than he looks!"

"Yes indeed. I did and I am!" smiled Yiannis proudly. "Right let's get you back to your hotel young man."

Andrew turned to Katerina, "Antio sas and efcharisto," he smiled at her warmly. "It has been such a lovely evening."

"Keep trying Andrew, with the Greek language and maybe one day your dreams of living here will be answered. You are doing so well and efcharisto mou, my pleasure."

Very soon Andrew was back at the Holiday Inn. He paused in Reception to look at the large screen tv. The world news was broadcasting but tonight diddly squat from Cyprus.

"Thank goodness we are now yesterday's news," he mouthed silently and with utter relief.

Next morning, 7.30 on the dot, Yiannis arrived outside the hotel in full running gear - red tee shirt and shorts and a bright red headband. Andrew joined him in his more conventional black tee shirt and white shorts.

"Okay Andrew, it's best we stick together as you don't know your way around. So, we will start by turning left, running through Metaxas Square then on to Paphos Street, Egypt Street, Stassinos Avenue which will bring us to the Turkish occupation. We will continue round the city walls until we reach Marcos Dracos Avenue then we will be back on Paphos Street."

"Sounds good, how long is that?"

"About 5.5 kilometres or 3.2 miles. If we just keep to the same pace we shouldn't encounter any problems but we have to be careful when we go through the Turkish half. Okay, let's go!"

They set off at a good pace and managed to keep together. Yiannis pointed out the different roads as they passed through. There were several Turkish soldiers who looked rather sternly at them and Andrew was more than a little concerned to note they all had a finger on their triggers.

Yiannis sensed his tension, "Just keep running Andrew and don't look at them!"

Andrew immediately did as the Chief advised and it was somewhat of a relief when they arrived safely back to Paphos Street and the Holiday Inn. He was pleased with the experience of his run round the city walls of Nicosia though.

"Efcharisto Yiannis, thank you so much," he beamed.

"That's fine Andrew, I enjoyed it too thank you! It has been too long since I last exercised this poor body of mine.

I am going home now to shower and change but I will be back here around 10.30. We will then go on to the American hospital and pick up our grizzly bear, Harry!"

Andrew went straight to his room, showered then went down to breakfast, both exhilarated and relieved Yiannis had accompanied him. He had worked up quite an appetite so ordered the full breakfast.

As he was leaving the flamboyant American CBS reporter approached him again, offering even more cash for his exclusive story.

"Look Sir, if you keep hassling me I will have you arrested and held in a cell at the Nicosia police station!"

The American backed away, holding up his hands as though a gun had just been pointed at him. "Okay young fella. I didn't mean to harass ya. I'm flying back to the States tomorrow, so just forget it son, forget it okay?"

At 10.30 Galanis arrived, Andrew went out the minute he spotted the car.

"Enjoy your long awaited run round our city walls then?"

"Oh, yes! Really exhilarating and enjoyable thank you Sir. I would love to come back and do it all again in the near future."

When they arrived at the American hospital, Doctor Ally Martizez met them and they followed him to the wards.

"How's Harry?" asked Andrew.

"Oh, I am pleased to report he is back on form now and joking with the nurses. Also he has been telling every man and his dog just how good Brighton is. I think he wants to give us a guided tour if ever we visit England!

He will have to keep the plaster on his head for at least four days but a week preferably, when his local hospital will remove his staples and probably do another chest X-ray. We will notify them.

Right let's go and see him - then you can take him away with our blessing!"

"Hi Harry," Andrew greeted him.

"Yes, hello Harry," added Chief Galanis. "So, I hear you are fully compos mentis now dear man?"

"Meaning?" Harry questioned with a grin.

"Meaning, yesterday you were making less sense than the Jabberwocky my son!"

"Lewis Carroll!" beamed Andrew, knowing that one.

"Yes, indeed Andrew."

"Okay, you two I do concede now - I don't think I was quite ready to leave here earlier."

"Hallelujah!" interjected Dr Ally. "Now gentlemen take him away, you have him, please!"

"How is my officer doctor?" asked Chief Galanis.

"I'm afraid we need to keep Xephyr in for a few more days yet, simply because of the acute infection, his thigh is taking quite a while to heal over, but that is only to be expected of course. I will take you to his ward."

Harry and Andrew went along too.

Xephyr was sitting in a chair next to his bed. He was pleased to see the Chief and the other two, though looked very pale and gaunt. They stayed a few minutes talking then Galanis said they had better go but he would call in again tomorrow. Xephyr smiled weakly then closed his eyes.

On the way back to the hotel Galanis said he would ask his secretary to confirm flights for them both to Gatwick tomorrow.

"She will phone you with your flight times and email or call Angela at your station to arrange for someone to meet you at Gatwick.

I will have a word with your DCS later, just to clarify a few things, I will also call in here tomorrow morning before you leave to say goodbye.

Take care both of you. I know the case hasn't closed for you yet at home but I hope you get a result soon after your return. Please keep me informed of any significant developments."

"We will Sir and efcharisto, thank you for yesterday's meal."

"No problem Andrew. Both Katerina and I enjoyed your company and she asked me to encourage you to continue with your Greek. She said it could soon be very useful to you, but I don't know why she said that."

"I do Sir, please thank her."

"Right, now the Chief has left Andrew I will just pop up to my room for a change of clothes then we will order a coffee and you can tell me everything about yesterday and your dinner with him."

It wasn't long before they were sat in the lounge enjoying their drinks and as they looked over Metaxas Square they noticed a huge market had set up, commandeering the whole carpark, so they decided to have a walk over later.

Harry was keen to buy a little something to take back for Liz. He had been thinking of her constantly while in his hospital bed. He realised only too well she had been long suffering and loyal for so long because of the nature of his work so he wanted to acknowledge just how much he appreciated her.

... Perhaps a Hermes scarf - she had always craved one for as long as he could remember but the prices were so utterly prohibitive ...

"Right, I'm all ears Andrew. Tell me everything I've missed!"

So Andrew recounted in detail: getting the bags of diamonds from the bank to the solicitor's plush offices; weighing them all individually on the precision scales; giving them a new, secure home in the solicitor's safe and how Galanis and himself were witnesses to both signatures.

"I did think about doing a runner as I was carrying the jewels though!" Harry looked at him open mouthed.

"Only joking Harry! The ladies thought it an amusing twist though. Anyway, as we were enjoying a drink in a nearby cafe after the work was done, Yiannis Galanis took a call from Ankara concerning Nico Castellanos - that's when you text back 'Hooray!' after I messaged you."

"Yes, that was the best news of the day!" Harry laughed. "I'll tell you something Andrew you have certainly developed a deeper confidence in yourself than you owned the first day I met you. I remember meeting a shy, blushing youngster less than a month ago and just look at you now - a confident detective able to mix with anyone at any level and execute your job to the highest degree. You should be so proud of yourself!"

"Well thank you Harry," Andrew beamed, "but I've one hell of a brilliant mentor!"

Andrew looked over at his boss, "You're not blushing are you Harry?"

"Cheeky monkey!" and they both broke into spontaneous laughter.

"It's so good to have you back Harry. I was lost here without you."

"Did Chief Galanis enlighten you at all on the nationalities of the two dead men?"

"Yes, he did. The man I shot was Andreas Athanasiou and he was a Greek Cypriot. He explained that had I killed Yirgos Papadopoulos, the one born in Bethnal Green, I would have had the Greek mafia after me back home. Is that right Harry?"

"Oh, yes Andrew! I'm afraid that's how they work and I've experienced their retribution myself!"

"Really? Can you tell me about it?"

"I'm afraid not, but I think you already know that! Working within the Special Branch we are not allowed to divulge any aspect of any of the cases we work on. You will learn all about that in time no doubt.

So, how did you come to be dining at Galanis's home?"

"Oh, yes. Well after our reports were written up he invited me to his house for dinner. A barbecue as it turned out. He and his wife Katerina have a lovely home and she was so welcoming. He even asked me to call him 'Yiannis' while we were there!

The meal was absolutely delicious but then came the surprise of the evening ..." Andrew paused for a while.

Harry was all ears.

"He asked me if he could join me on a run the next morning! You could have knocked me down with a feather! He kept up with me too! Apparently he ran in a few of the Greek marathons. Can you believe it?"

Harry shook his head. "Where did you go?"

"All round the city walls. Running through the Turkish half was a bit scary though! Do you know the Turkish guards have their fingers poised on the triggers of the guns the moment anyone passes?"

Harry nodded his head. "Yes, it's common practice."

"Anyway, I was safely back at the hotel having breakfast when this persistent American reporter hassled me for the second time wanting information on the shootings but I shook him off."

"Good for you Andrew doing the right thing! I am so pleased you have people trusting in you. You are so sincere and helpful with everyone, as I complemented you earlier, a fine, confident, upright young man." Harry looked at his watch. "Right, let's go over and have a wander through the market before it packs away. Keep close together though, just in case of any trouble. I can't be dealing with anymore!"

Walking round the stalls Harry attracted a lot of attention - after all no one else there was sporting a huge white plaster perched on the back of their head!

"You really need to buy a hat Harry ... look there's a wide brimmed Panama one over on that stall. That will cover your plaster!"

Harry tried it on. "Ummm, it's a good fit now but will be much too big when it's just covering my head soon. Oh, it's not a bad price though, I'll take it."

Andrew was taken with a Cyprus tee shirt and very soon Harry came across a very classy Hermes scarf for Liz.

"Right, I think we've done here then Andrew?" Andrew nodded so they made their way back to the hotel for a late lunch and refreshing drink.

"I must ring my parents to let them know we have a flight back to Gatwick sometime tomorrow."

They had only just ordered lunch when Andrew's phone rang. It was Sophia, Galanis's secretary.

"Yassou Sophia."

"Yassou to you too Andrew," she laughed.

"I am calling to say I have booked you both on an Easy Jet flight from Larnaca to Gatwick tomorrow at 12.15pm. Arrival time in the UK being 2.15pm. Chief Galanis has arranged for a car to take you to Larnaca airport. Pick up time from your hotel will be at 10am.

I have called your DCS's secretary, Angela, and she is arranging for a driver called Bob to meet you at Gatwick. She is lovely to talk to and I think she is missing you both!"

"Efcharisto, thanks Sophia," Andrew acknowledged.

"And my thanks to you too Andrew! Please keep up with learning our language."

"Well, all sorted then," sighed Harry, "home tomorrow. I will give Liz a call later ... but I was just thinking about having a special meal out tonight in Ledra Street, what say you?"

Andrew's eyes beamed.

"Yes, at the Romanzo Taverna, I think judging by your face, you've already guessed it Andrew! I can say my goodbyes to my friend Zaikai then."

"Don't you mean 'Antio sas' Harry? And yes, I would love to. We might get a lift back to the hotel in Zaikai's Aston Martin again too!" he drooled.

"Okay Andrew, sorted! I think we should have a restful afternoon and pack our bags ready for the morning."

At 5pm Harry knocked on Andrew's door. "Okay to go?"

"Yes. I've rung home, packed and had a good rest. Oh! and had a few words with myself, just for old times sake in the full length mirror on the wall!"

Harry looked at him bewildered.

"I may tell you about it one day Harry - but only if you promise not to laugh!"

None the wiser, Harry donned his Panama hat and they took a leisurely walk round Metaxas Square and down Ledra Street. As they approached the restaurant Zaikai spotted them and ran over to Harry, giving him the mother of all bear hugs! Harry's hat toppled off during the embrace disclosing the ginormous plaster on the back of his head.

"It **was** you Harry on the news channel! I thought it might be! I will find you a table by the window my friend. And ... to cheer you up Harry, today we have on the menu my Specialty Moussaka with a dressed Greek salad. Would you both like that?"

Their faces said it all ... "and a large Keo and iced Coke please."

"No problem Harry and Andrew. It's such a pleasure to see you both again. How much longer will you be here?"

"It's our last night Zaikai. We fly home tomorrow."

"Then I will make this very special for you."

A waiter brought their drinks. Andrew raised his glass and said, "Yamas, cheers to you Harry! I am so sad we are going back, but perhaps I may come for a holiday sometime."

The moussaka was absolutely delicious and as they cleaned their plates Zaikai came over and sat talking with them.

"Would you both like the baklava?" he asked. Once again their faces answered for them.

"You must have a Metaxa with me too Harry!" he declared. Food and drinks demolished Zaikai proudly announced he would give them a lift back to the hotel ... Harry and Andrew waited outside for him with baited breath ... when "WHAT ... the??"

... Low and behold a beaten up old American jeep that looked as though it had been used for target practice came chug, chugging around the corner with Zaikai at the helm.

"What's this?" croaked Andrew. "No Aston Martin?" as he picked his chin up from the gutter.

"Sorry chaps! We have been attracting some young gangs around here lately, getting their kicks by scratching cars they are, so the Aston is under lock and key for the immediate future."

The kindest euphemism to describe their bone shaking journey back to the hotel in the old jeep was 'a bit of a bumpy ride', but it got them back to the Holiday Inn safely. Zaikai gave both Harry and Andrew big hugs and said he wanted to see them in Cyprus again soon.

"Yes, we hope so too. But for now, efcharisto and kalinychta."

"Very good Andrew!" Zaikai's words carried across the cool night air as he drove off.

Next morning at breakfast Harry confessed he hadn't slept much last night, so would try to grab a nap on the plane.

Their DCS and Chief Galanis had gone halves on their bill so they just collected their passports from Reception and went out to the waiting police car. Galanis pulled up to say 'goodbye'. He also had an interesting update for them ...

It concerned Dimitris Pantazis's personal possessions. It had remained a mystery as to why he'd had absolutely no form of identification on him when his body was discovered on Brighton Beach.

The Chief had asked his officers to search the farmhouse and it's outbuildings thoroughly the days following the shootings. After probing around the old machinery two officers discovered a dustbin which had obviously been used to burn papers. They turned it upside down and there among the embers were parts of a badly charred passport.

Some of the letters were just visible though: 'mit' ... 'nta' ... 'is'.

Also on further investigation of an outbuilding they noticed a shelf holding stacks of old saucepan lids absolutely riddled with bullet holes. They went over for a closer inspection and there among the lids was a mobile phone with a bullet hole right through the centre which had rendered it impossible to trace of course.

The police officers agreed they must have been darned accurate marksmen.

Chief Galanis sent details of the make, model and colour to Mrs Sakalis who confirmed it was Dimitris'. They had obviously taken the items from his pockets after they shot him to make identification near impossible.

"So, yesterday," concluded Chief Galanis, "the National Passport Office, confirmed the charred pieces we sent to them were definitely from the passport of Dimitris Pantazis.

So Harry and Andrew, two more pieces of your puzzle have slotted into place, yes?"

"Thank you so much Chief for your dedication and help with this matter," said Harry.

Galanis smiled, gave his shoulders a little shrug and told them, "Stay in touch now!"

"Oh we will," and they waved until the Chief was out of sight.

"I wonder if Angela has got anywhere yet with her enquiries?" Andrew pondered, already moving on to just who the potential diamond smugglers could be back in Brighton …

Chapter 16

Still waters run deep

–A quiet or placid manner may conceal a more passionate or volatile nature, concealed deep within ...

Harry smiled inwardly with a great deal of satisfaction. He could certainly see much of his younger self in his young prodigy here.

"So Andrew, who do you feel is behind the diamond smuggling racket back home?"

"Well, I certainly think it's a female Harry and my best bet would be the deceased Winnie Williams."

"Oh, why?" asked Harry.

"There are so many clues."

Harry remained silent, so Andrew continued ...

"She had Dimitris Pantazis's name in her address book; she didn't own up to knowing him after the shooting; she was a mistress of disguise - changing her appearance, often on a twice daily basis; she probably became too greedy and that's why 'The Black Ford Two' beat her up ... and ... I'm sure you are aware of this too Harry, that flat she lives in so close to the seafront is in a highly desirable area. It must be worth an absolute fortune, so that lady was certainly not poor.

I rest my case!"

"Hmmmmm! It's a thought but I have an alternative scenario to put to you. I like you think it is a lady." Harry paused for a moment going into one of his reveries ...

"My money however is on Max's wife, Jane Grey."

"Why? What evidence is there against her?"

"None! None whatsoever."

"I don't follow you Harry."

"Sometimes Andrew, you just have to go with your gut. As I have said before, 'Still waters run deep', a quiet or seemingly placid person may conceal a more passionate or volatile nature kept hidden well within. Also she has darned easy access to those cars."

"But, and a very big 'but' Harry - her husband was very nearly shot dead by who you are saying would have been her co conspirators - 'The Black Ford Two'.

... So, to sum up - I have tangible facts and you have your grumbling gut?" he sniggered playfully.

Harry nodded, smiling - and a very cheeky smile it was too.

"Would you like to place a friendly wager on who's right?"

Harry nodded with that cheeky smile again, "Yes!! and as you have called it a friendly wager Andrew, I bet you a glass of beer - which you must drink if you loose to a pint of Coke - which I must drink if I loose. Agreed?"

"Agreed!"

"Ha ha! I'm just longing to see your face after you take your first sip of beer!"

"That will **never** happen!"

"Oh it will!"

"Won't!"

"Will ..."

Chapter 17

Crime and Punishment

Everything ran smoothly at the airport and very soon they had boarded the aircraft and were awaiting takeoff. Harry had given Andrew the window seat so he could take a last look at the Pyrenees. Andrew was utterly made up by his kind gesture.

After an early coffee and sandwiches Harry warily conceded a sleep was in order.

"Oh, yes okay. But first could I hear a little of your background, I told you mine earlier. Also how did you come to be a Detective Chief Inspector?"

"Okay Andrew I do of course owe you that! Well, starting at the beginning ... I am an only child from the East End of London, Shoreditch. My mother was an office cleaner, my father worked in the old Spitalfields market. I enjoyed helping him at weekends and during school holidays.

I left school with 3 'A' levels and 4 'O' levels. I didn't fancy going to college or university - sitting behind a desk was definitely not my bag so I helped dad in the market full time.

This was fine until," Harry took a little gulp and closed his eyes tightly for a moment or two, very wary of the shame he was about to expose to Andrew ... "until I got mixed up with a group of boys who delighted in nicking cars and going joy riding. I helped with the unlocking of doors and getting the vehicles started. All this was fun until one evening I was too ill with flu to go out with them. Well, my Illness was fortuitous for me as it transpired, you see that night they all got caught in a police trap and each of them received a six month prison sentence."

Andrew gasped, utterly speechless.

" ... My dad found out everything soon after and I got a hefty clip around the ear. He told me I'd had a lucky break but any behaviour like that in the future would be devastating, the end of any decent career prospects.

Have you ever heard of Fyodor Dostoevsky's Crime and Punishment?"

Andrew nodded ... "But I haven't read it," he added quickly.

"Well, just to underline the fact to me, dad dragged me off to see a mate of his, a prison officer in Belmarsh prison. It scared me rigid walking through those heavy iron doors - I certainly didn't want to end up in there, so, in a nutshell, no more crime for me and no more punishment.

Dad's friend persuaded me to join the Police Cadets. I'll tell you what Andrew, that was the best U-turn I ever made! I passed all my exams and like you went to Hendon and then on to the Metropolitan. After a year they asked me to join the Special Branch."

He looked over to Andrew and smiled, "That's how my skills with opening doors and starting cars both originated and came in useful!" he confessed.

Andrew smiled back.

Harry then continued, "My dad became ill with cancer and unfortunately died at the age of 57. My mother was forced to give up her cleaning job to look after him and became quite exhausted towards the end. I think she lost the will to live after he died and she passed away just a little while later. It was all quite sad.

I remained with the Special Branch for as long as I could but after ten years it is mandatory to go back to a station as you probably know.

One of the best moves of my life Andrew was when I then married Liz. We wanted to live by the coast so moved to Brighton and it has been a good life there ever since. So, there you have it Andrew - Harry Webb's somewhat checkered past!"

"Wow Harry, I was just not expecting that! Incredible! So could you also explain in more detail how you came to be shot in the chest three times?"

"Oh, ten out of ten for trying Andrew but as I have told you before, I cannot divulge or discuss any Special Branch matters with another soul - ever!" With that he yawned wearily.

"I'm sorry Andrew but I really am exhausted now, probably the after effects of that bang on the head and strong medication but before I do go off to the land of Nod I just have to compliment you again on your excellent shooting back at the farm. Absolutely brilliant! I leave you now, however, to think about our first move when we return to Brighton ..."

While Harry was deep in the heart of Nod, Andrew gazed longingly out of the window, absolutely mesmerised by the beauty of the Pyrenees and wishing he was there. The flight went not only smoothly but quickly too and very soon Andrew was gently nudging Harry in the ribs until he eventually awoke.

"Oooow, where are we Andrew?" he asked drowsily. "Just about to land at Gatwick Harry."

"Crikey days, I must have needed that sleep!" he exclaimed.

Very soon they were outside the airport looking out for Bob. No sooner did they do so than he magically turned up just like a magician's dove.

"Good t'see you both again," he grinned, "'ad a good 'oliday 'av you? Only jokin' 'cos we 'eard reports on Auntie's News 'an guessed it was you two."

"We're fine thanks Bob," replied Harry taking off his Panama hat.

"Gordon Bennett 'arry! What you bin un done?" Bob asked on clocking his plaster.

"Well, suffice to say Bob I had quite a vicious misunderstanding with a ruddy great boulder - and the ruddy great boulder won!"

"Ohhhhh! Yeh, looks like it did too mate!"

"So, how are things back at the station Bob?"

"All okay 'arry. Just the odd tea leaves and speeding cars. No one brought any cars to me wiv sparklers behind their radios though!"

Harry laughed.

"Oh look - 'arry - a lovely lady waiting for ya outside yer 'ouse!"

"Liz, Liz!"

Harry was out of the car in a trice and while Bob collected his holdall from the boot Liz gave her husband a long, loving hug - then she suddenly noticed his plaster.

She gave him another extra sympathetic hug. Andrew popped out of the car to say hello and he was given a big hug too.

"My word, the lawn is looking good Liz, have you mown it?"

"Oh no Harry - I got a man in!"

As Harry was still gulping open mouthed Liz added, "... and before you go Andrew, DCS Street wants you both to meet him in the office for a meeting at 9am."

"No rest for the wicked," quipped Andrew.

"See you early in the morning then," smiled Harry.

"Yes, I'll give DCS Street a ring before Bob drops me off. See you tomorrow Harry, bye!"

Liz took Harry's holdall, "Right, my injured soldier, let's have a cup of tea and you can tell me all about your adventures in Cyprus!"

"Okay Liz - but first please make my day and say you have a lemon drizzle cake in there fresh from the oven?"

"But of course Harry - I know you so well!"

"Oh it's really lovely to be home ... so who's this man you've got in then?"

Meanwhile, back in the car, Andrew rang the DCS to confirm they were both fine with the 9pm meeting.

"That's good," John Street acknowledged, "but Andrew could you make it a little earlier please? I have something rather important I would like to ask you in private."

"No problem Sir. I planned on getting up early anyway to take a run along the promenade."

Next morning Andrew took his early morning run and quite literally bumped into Julian and John, the two paramedics. They were pleased to see each other and exchanged pleasantries as they passed.

Andrew was soon in the DCS's office, wondering what on earth was wanted of him. He didn't have to wait for long however before he was silently listening to what John Street proposed.

... Well, he certainly was not expecting that!

Although still quite stunned he immediately accepted the proposition the DCS had put to him.

"Keep this to yourself for now though Andrew. I want to tell the others when everyone's together."

Andrew nodded, his mind rather numb.

Harry arrived soon after to a tumultuous cheer from the other officers.

"Well done again to you both! We all guessed it was you two on the BBC news!"

"Thanks chaps, but after all it's only part of the job!" Harry smiled in his usual diplomatic manner.

At that point Angela arrived and gave them both an affectionate hug.

DCS Street then called all three into his office.

"First and foremost welcome back you two! Thank you for keeping both Angela and myself well informed throughout. I am delighted it was a good result in so many diverse ways. The murderers are now dead themselves and Nico Castellanos won't be worrying anyone for a very long time.

But now, back to work! Well, I am pleased to inform you Angela has been most diligent with her research while you were away, so, over to you Angela, explain all!"

"Thank you Sir. Well Harry, as you asked me to be your deputy while you were in Cyprus, my first port of call took me to the Old Ship, to have a light lunch and as requested an interview with Eugene Demirci the waiter.

He was very keen to talk as he was feeling really raw and upset by Winnie's brutal death. I asked him if he could give me some information about himself also his reason for coming to Brighton. This is what he told me and I quote:

"'Well, you probably know I'm a Turkish Cypriot and I have been living in England for about twenty years. I started work in a London restaurant, stayed there for five years then moved to Brighton. I love working here and have a flat at the back of the hotel. The staff are all very friendly.

I go back to Cyprus about three times a year and stay with my cousin in Famagusta as my parents were both killed in the Turkish military invasion back in 1974. They had a farm which is still standing in the unoccupied village in the green buffer zone. It brings back such bad memories though.

The main reason for returning every year is I take what money I have saved from my wages to distribute to the orphans living around the village outskirts. It's something I really enjoy doing as it makes me feel good inside, a little like a summer Father Christmas!

He smiled rather shyly at this point and I thanked him. He said he hoped I would go back for lunch one day as it was good to talk.

I crossed him off my list of possible suspects as I believed every word he spoke. He really is a most genuine, kind person!"

"Brilliant work Angela!" commended John Street, and they nodded in agreement.

"The next day I walked along the promenade to the apartment where Winnie Williams had lived. The first thing I noticed was the 'For Sale' board, so I called the agent as I was curious to know the asking price. I was surprised to hear it was a whopping £580,000! I thought about this and wondered how she could live in such an expensive apartment and yet have to go begging several times a week. It didn't make sense."

At this juncture Andrew leaned forward and smiled across at Harry, feeling quite smug. Harry shook his head dismissively in response.

"I decided then to knock on number 7 for a word with her neighbour and friend Mary Mills," continued Angela. "She was only too pleased to speak to me and put the kettle on.

She wanted me to pass on her thanks to Harry for all the help he gave in finding her a care assistant. She said to pass on too that she was feeling much better now, her leg had healed and she didn't need crutches anymore. So Harry I'm passing on her best wishes to you now."

Harry smiled a 'thank you'.

"I then asked Mary for some information on Winnie to help us with our enquiries. I mentioned her sister, Linda Bowman had said in an interview that Winnie was struggling financially so did she believe this to be correct?

She explained Winnie's husband had died about 15 months ago. I didn't realise she had been married but Barry, her husband, was apparently a very friendly man and would often take them both out for the day to places like Hastings, Arundel, Portsmouth and on occasion to London.

He was an extremely careful driver so when police called to say he was killed in a road traffic accident on the Bexhill Road, Winnie would not accept it. The police said he skidded off the road, hit a tree from which the impact almost sliced his car in half!

I asked if there were any witnesses or dash cam photos but she didn't know and suggested I ask her sister, Linda Bowman about that.

I must emphasise here Mary's mind does tend to wander for miles so I had to try hard to keep her focused. I asked her again quite specifically of Winnie's financial position. She became flustered and again suggested I should ask Linda, but then suddenly remembered she herself had witnessed both Winnie's and her husband's signatures on a mortgage release form for the sale of a larger house on 5th Avenue so was mortgage free on her apartment.

Mr Williams had been a freelance salesman selling mens suits to department stores like Hepworths, Debenhams and House of Fraser, all of which do not even exist anymore. Oh, he also prided himself on always being immaculately dressed.

Winnie worked in Dorothy Perkins as a sales assistant so that's probably where she met Barry. She did not work after he died so just had a small pension to live on along with the pittance she earned helping Tom the deckchair attendant.

Obviously Mary had no clue Winnie was actually out begging. I said my goodbyes and left."

At this juncture Angela looked up and sighed, "So I didn't feel I had really achieved much there and decided I should make a follow up call to Winnie's sister and brother in law in Littlehampton.

I had some urgent office work to catch up on so decided to take the 700 bus to Littlehampton on Saturday afternoon. I also thought I would have a better chance of catching them both at home then. It was quite easy to locate them as there was a blue van parked outside with yellow lettering on the front and back - CAR SPARES DELIVERED call: 07778 7678149.

A man was looking under the van's bonnet so I stood back and waited a couple of minutes until he eventually looked up and saw me.

'Are you Mr Bowman?' I asked, he relied, 'Yes can I help you?'

So I showed him my police card and asked if his wife was at home as I would like to ask some questions regarding her late sister Winnie. Linda was pleased to see me, hoped she could be of help and told me to call them Linda and Clive.

The first thing she asked was whether the two men shot dead in Cyprus were the two who beat up and killed her sister, so I did confirm that. She asked no more questions about them though.

I told her I'd had a few words with Mary and also I had noticed the 'For Sale' board on Winnie's apartment.

She told me the probate was now completed and as there was no mortgage on the property they instructed their solicitor to sell it. She asked if I was interested in buying but I laughed and told her I was happy with my basement flat just five minutes walk from the police station.

I asked her about Winnie's husband being in the fatal road accident on the A529 at which point they both looked at each other knowingly. Clive explained he often took that route too and no matter how bad the weather conditions were, Barry would have easily coped with them. He was a careful driver and would never have approached that bend with speed.

They asked the police if any other traffic was around at the time but there wasn't only the lorry driver who was first on the scene and had dialled 999, but he told police a black Ford car came speeding by him with two men inside and he wondered if they were involved in anyway."

"What!" shouted the DCS, sentiments echoed loudly by both Harry and Andrew, "Why the hell weren't we informed of this? Angela, get me the file please, immediately!"

DCS Street read aloud text from the file of the fatal RTA which stated the lorry driver was duly questioned by police and asked to hand over his dash cam footage. Unfortunately though his camera was in for repair so was not not working that night. No other witnesses were on the scene.

"Okay, Angela, what more did you find out from the Bowman's?" he sighed disappointedly.

"I asked Clive if he was still supplying Mr Grey at the Classic Cars garage. He explained he was but they were a relatively small customer only requiring plugs and windscreen wipers for the MGBs. I asked if he encountered any difficulties regarding payments from him and he confirmed yes, he had recently and heard other suppliers were not being paid either.

Then, going back to Winnie's apartment, I told them I didn't want to pry but asked if they had any thoughts on what to do with the money. They had actually considered it and Clive planned an early retirement as his business wasn't paying well.

Linda, who works in an old people's home wanted to make a donation of a colour television to them as their old one was small and unreliable. Their daughter works in India looking after injured children and has just one more year out there so will need somewhere to live when she returns.

Linda at that point became quite tearful, saying money wasn't everything and given the choice they would rather remain poor and have Winnie back with them. I thanked them both, left to catch the 700 bus home and crossed them off my list.

My next task on your list Harry was to question Mr and Mrs Grey, but before I did so I wanted a word with Bob in our compound as I was still curious about the small bags of diamonds he retrieved from behind the radios in the MGB cars. Why just MGBs I wondered? So, to satisfy my own curiosity I needed to know just what size the bag could be to be hidden behind a radio, or anywhere else in a vehicle come to that.

Bob obligingly opened the bonnet of a Ford Focus 1.6; we looked in; then in the boot; under the spare wheel and under the carpet. Point made I had to agree with him it just wasn't feasible to hide them in any of those places in that car.

He explained in modern cars the radio is all part of the dashboard and not easy to remove. Then he laughingly suggested, unless anyone possessed keys like Harry's of course!

Next he took me to an old Citroen car and showed me the four small screws that could easily be removed to take the radio out. It was similar to that of the MGB's apparently. Of course if Harry hadn't tried the radio while bringing it to the compound and smelt a rat when it wouldn't work, the diamonds would never have been discovered ... I understood all now!

When I returned to my office I looked through your reports and noticed the day you interviewed the two mechanics, Stan and Alex there should have been a third man working alongside them but he was off sick. I wanted to find out more about him.

I phoned the garage and spoke to Stan. I asked him who the third mechanic was. He was a man by the name of Eric Delaney, their electrician responsible for rewiring the MGBs. 'Eric the Lec' they nicknamed him. Apparently Mrs Grey had specifically asked that Eric personally should always take the MGBs to the Gatwick workshop to be fitted with the 6 speaker surround sound systems.

Interestingly he hadn't turned up for work since being off sick.

So, I asked Stan for his number. He said I could try it but held little hope of me getting any reply. He had tried ringing many times himself, even driven over to his flat on the outskirts of Gatwick. He always knocked loudly on his front door but no one ever answered.

The lady from next door, however, had popped her head over the wall on the last occasion and told him he had up and left one night, without paying his rent or giving anyone a forwarding address. Vanished just like that he had in a puff of smoke. There one minute ... gone the next!"

Angela paused for breath, took a few sips of water then continued:

"My next task was to visit Mr and Mrs Grey so I phoned the Classic Cars garage where Stan answered. He explained Max was out on other business and I asked him how Mr Grey and the garage were fairing now. Well, badly as it transpired!

Trade was down, overheads up, customers had dwindled away and he was almost certain Mr Grey had been gambling heavily at the late night casinos.

Mrs Grey, meanwhile had commandeered every aspect of the accounting. She appeared to be making all major company decisions too. Max, to all and sundry was a lost soul.

I have been thinking for awhile Mrs Grey was a main suspect regarding working alongside Nico Castellanos also likely to be the lady responsible for phoning the Holiday Inn at Nicosia to ask for your room number Harry."

At this juncture Harry looked over to Andrew who quite deliberately kept his head down avoiding his gaze ...

"So I thought to myself 'What would Harry do next?' and the answer came quite telepathically I believe ... 'Use the services of those in the know' so I rang Elaine the Easy Jet superintendent as she helped you by going through the departures list to Larnaca, giving you the names of Yirgos Papadopoulos and Andreas Athanasiou.

When I rang she sounded very pleasant and really wanted to be of service. She felt it her duty to help the police.

I told her I needed any details of a Mr Castellanos and a Mrs Jane Grey flying to Larnaca Airport, Cyprus or possibly by Ataturk to Istanbul Airport Turkey during the last six months. I remembered Andrew had a photo of Nico Castellanos taken at The Grand while having dinner with Mr Dimitris Pantazis so I emailed a copy of that to her.

Elaine explained it could normally take a really long time to source this type of information but I could be in luck as she had two students with her on Work Experience at the moment who both seemed very keen to learn all aspects of the job. She would assign one of them to the Departures area looking at all CCTV coverage and the other searching through all the boarding passes between those dates.

And that gentlemen, is where we stand at present," Angela concluded.

"Thanks Angela, I am so impressed with the hours you devoted to this and to your quality of work!" commended DCS Street.

"Yes, sending the photograph of Nico Castellanos was most impressive," Andrew praised her.

"We should make you a special detective," Harry quipped.

"Well, maybe we will!" added John Street.

"No thanks gentlemen, I am more than happy as I am thank you very much. No way could I cope with your hours and commitments! You are all a very special breed indeed!"

Just then her office phone rang so she left to answer it.

"Y E S !" she suddenly shouted out with excitement. "Thank you Elaine that is wonderful news, I just cannot thank you enough! ... Oh, and please thank your students too, I expect they are blurry eyed after three days of searching through boarding passes and CCTV footage."

"They are okay Angela I think they enjoyed the challenge. The beer money they earned was quite an incentive too!" replied Elaine.

"I'm just sending everything through to you now Angela. Bye for now and if you ever fly from here please give me a call and we will have a drink together."

"Yes, I certainly will Elaine!"

Angela quickly returned to the DCS's office. "Well, you no doubt heard my excitement Sir. Elaine's students have cracked it! We now have it on record Mrs Jane Grey and Mr Nico Castellanos travelled together on an Easy Jet flight to Larnaca, Cyprus - flight number: 4681, seats J32 and J33.

They also travelled on an Easy Jet flight to Istanbul, Turkey - flight number: 9887, seats H44 and H45! Yes, Yes, Yes!"

"Thank you Angela, you have excelled yourself! This case is now well on its way to nearing a most satisfactory conclusion," praised John Street.

"Well Harry if you are up to it can you both call on Mrs Grey immediately?"

"On our way Sir," their voices echoed as they shot off.

Andrew went to the compound, brought round Harry's BMW and off they sped.

"Call in at the Classic Cars garage first Andrew. We need to have a word with Max Grey first I believe, to make sure his wife will be at home."

Andrew put his foot down and soon they arrived at the garage. They pulled onto the forecourt only to find flags hung all over the showroom and 'All Cars for Sale' banners draped over vehicles and pasted on the windows.

Max saw them pull up and went outside to greet them. "Hello you two, have you come for the sale then? Can I interest you in this little beauty?" he asked, directing his gaze at Harry. That beauty was indeed a gleaming red MGB.

"Urm, Max, I really, really love that car, in fact I am salivating over it but unfortunately that is not why we are here I'm afraid. We urgently need to have a few words with Mrs Grey, do you know if she is at home by any chance?"

"Well, to be honest with you I didn't see her this morning. We have been having a few problems of late so are sleeping in separate rooms now and I didn't get in until about 4am. There hasn't been much conversation between us of late either unfortunately.

... Strangely though I did try ringing her both at home and on her mobile this morning but got no reply. I put it down to her still being cross with me as she didn't answer my texts either," he sighed.

"Tell you what I will leave Stan in charge here and follow you to my place." He was now looking and sounding quite concerned.

Andrew set off as fast as he dared with Max Grey hot on his heels and virtually tailgating him for the duration of the journey. As the two cars screeched up the drive they saw Mrs Grey's car was parked up by the side door.

"That's just where it was this morning!" shouted Max frantically as he jumped out and threw open the front door.

"Jane, Jane!" he yelled as he rushed through the hallway. Harry and Andrew followed him into the lounge. There was an eerie stillness to the house ...

Max then brushed passed them as he backtracked along the hallway and went flying up the stairs two at a time.

"Jane, Jane!" he called, then, "Jane, oh no, no! Why oh why?" he sobbed taking her hand.

Harry and Andrew rushed up the stairs and into the master bedroom where Max was on his knees, utterly bereft and just repeating, "Why why, why?"

Scattered over the dressing table were several empty pill bottles.

Harry rang for an ambulance while Andrew checked for a pulse. There wasn't one but nevertheless he turned her onto her side and into the recovery position, thumping her back and doing chest compressions then checking for a pulse again.

He repeatedly did this until he had to tell Max, "Sorry Sir, it's too late I'm afraid. I really don't think the paramedics will be able to revive her either."

At this Harry took him by the arm and encouraged him, "Come on Max, let's go downstairs. I will get you a cup of tea or something stronger."

At that juncture the ambulance arrived and the paramedics rushed in. They confirmed Jane Grey was dead, presumably through a massive overdose of a cocktail of pills.

Almost immediately another ambulance that happened to be in the vicinity pulled up to offer assistance. Out jumped John and Julian.

"We meet again Andrew!"

"Yes, on my morning run, now here."

It was agreed the first two paramedics would take Mrs Jane Grey to the mortuary for a forensic examination while John and Julian stayed with Max until he was well enough to be left. Harry and Andrew decided it best to stay for a while too.

As the paramedics were moving Mrs Grey from the bed an envelope fell to the floor. John picked it up ... It just had 'Max' written on the front. John passed it over to him. Max started to read it then crumbled in a heap, silently sobbing.

Harry took it gently from his hand.

Max

This is now my only way out as I both loath and detest you! I was so in love with Nico – we were going to live together in Turkey, but now he will be imprisoned there for at least 15 years. I'm devastated as he meant the world to me.

It wasn't my job to keep our business going, but you, you selfish numskull, just go to casinos and gamble away the money. I'm meant to be a trophy on your arm not a common worker! The business is lost, we owe far more than your poxy garage is actually worth.

Nico was a real businessman. When things started to get dodgy with his partnership in Cyprus he had the foresight to skim diamonds off the firm and bring them over here making hundreds of thousands of pounds.

Eric Delaney would then take them to the surround sound unit at Gatwick to be safely banked behind the MGB's radios until they could be sold to private buyers - at a massive profit too! And you couldn't even see this going on under your own nose!

I don't know why I ever married you - you are a wretched, contemptible and absolutely useless husband. You've never provided adequately for me. Whereas Nico, bless him, gave me rare, flawless diamonds from De Beers no less. He knew how to treat a lady!

It should be you who's dead but that pair of hitmen Nico employed to kill you were as pathetic as you - missing your heart and hitting you in the shoulder!

Trust you to play dead and save your own skin! You have ruined everything - worm!

Harry tried to console him but Max just kept sobbing. He phoned the office and spoke to Angela ...

... "So it was probably her who phoned the Holiday Inn then?"

"Oh, without a doubt Angela. Andrew and I will stay here for a while until Max is settled. I'm just going round to ask the neighbours if they would be able to help him, if need be.

Can you keep the DCS informed please? The ambulance carrying Mrs Jane Grey's body has just left for the Royal Sussex hospital mortuary."

"Of course Harry."

"Max, is there a neighbour I could ask to pop by and see you later?"

"Oh, oh, yes please. Mr and Mrs Adams two doors down."

"Okay, I'll go and ask them now. Meanwhile Andrew will make you another cup of tea and if I were you I'd follow it with a whiskey chaser!"

Harry showed Mr and Mrs Adams his ID card. They were shocked when he briefed them on what had happened. They had seen the ambulances of course but ... "Oh, oh no! What a thing to happen to a neighbour. It didn't bear thinking about," they confessed.

"Yes, of course we will go round just as soon as we see you leave."

After an hour or so Max seemed much calmer, so much so Harry and Andrew were able to talk to him rationally about his business.

"Well, it's already on the market. I've been a bloody fool gambling away our money. This isn't an excuse, but I could tell Jane was loosing interest in me way before that, though I never guessed there was another man, no not another man! She told me many couples slept in separate bedrooms ... even the Queen and the Duke.

So who is this Nico?"

"Nico Castellanos or as you know him, Bert Barber of the surround sound systems."

"What? No, no!" he kept repeating.

"Well, unlike him I do not have a penny to my name - the next bet I always believed was going to be the big one but of course it never was ... what can I do Harry?"

"Well, first and foremost help yourself by getting professional advice on your gambling addiction. That is a no brainer!

My advice then would be to sell the garage quickly for the best price you can get. You are a good salesman and have quality cars in absolute pristine condition on that forecourt of yours. I'm sure you could sell those pretty darn quick too!

Also ... just a little lateral thinking here Max but after probate you will be the sole owner of a cache of flawless diamonds from De Beers I believe, thanks to Nico Castellanos! 'Flawless' are the top grade and if you need advice on selling them I know just the two ladies who could help you!

This would give you the means to provide a decent redundancy package for Stan and Alex who have been loyal to you over the years. You would also be in the position to repay any firms and individuals you may be indebted to."

"Oh, thank you so much Harry! Thank you! Thank you! I can see my way out now. I was so ashamed of not being able to settle my debts or pay my staff. Troubles just escalated then imploded on me.

Regrettably, betting made sense to my troubled mind as I stupidly believed it could have been a pathway out for me but I can clearly find my way through now and will never bet again as long as I live! I will still take your advice though and seek professional help, just to be on the safe side.

Talking helps, it really does. You two have been marvellous. Thank you! Thank you so much!"

"Just look after yourself Max and take all the help you are offered. Both ambulance crews have left here now and you seem well in control of yourself so if it's okay with you Andrew and I will go too. Mr and Mrs Adams will be round shortly so please tell them of any needs or concerns you still have. As you so rightly said, it really does help to talk. They seem a lovely couple."

"They are and thank you both so much once again. Thank you."

Chapter 18

DRINK ME!!

"Result!" announced DCS John Street at the following morning's meeting. "Very well done everyone, I can now close this case!"

"Well Sir, the only small point we could not answer was why is Mr Dimitris Pantazis's phone number in Winnie Williams' note book?"

"I know you are a stickler for the minutest detail Harry, but I think you must accept it will be one of those minor irritations that may remain unexplained I'm afraid. Everything else is tied up beautifully!" he smiled.

"Now Angela, is everything on record?"

"Yes Sir, and all backed up on the cloud!"

"Thanks again and thanks too for the work you put in at Harry's request while he and Andrew were away in Cyprus." he smiled at her.

"I have been wondering for a while Harry why the two men wanted to kidnap you on your immediate arrival in Cyprus, albeit they took the wrong man!" he nodded towards Andrew.

"It was most probably instigated by Nico Castellanos Sir. He was in league with Mrs Jane Grey who I believe phoned the hotel the evening of our arrival to ascertain we were staying there then to obtain my room number.

We also know he hired the two crooks who abducted Andrew and who killed Mr Dimitris Pantazis. He was also responsible for the deaths of Winnie and probably countless others including both Mrs Angie Sakalis's husband and Winnie Williams' husband.

I still have a few enemies from my London days in the Special Branch but as you know I cannot divulge further information regarding that Sir. Suffice to say there are still people both here and Cyprus wanting me dead as revenge for me putting their partners behind bars."

"Too true Harry! I did have a conversation with your Commanding Officer who gave me the briefest of outlines, in the strictest confidence may I add. I can tell you now I would never want to endure what you have gone through for your work." He sat forward in his chair ...

"So are we all in agreement, case now closed?"

"Agreed," echoed the votes of approval.

"Okay, good. Now if you will come out to the main office I have a very important announcement to make."

DCS John Street tapped his pen on a glass to get everyone's attention ...

"The first thing I would like to say is the announcement I am about to make is in the strictest confidence. You have all taken the Law Enforcement Oath of Honour, now, with that in mind I am asking for your utter secrecy in never repeating the following information outside of this office:

Okay. Most of you know Harry and Andrew, with some recent help from Angela have been working on the case of the Cypriot gentleman, Mr Dimitris Pantazis who was shot dead on our Brighton beach, also the case of Mrs Winnie Williams who died as a result of a subsequent violent attack on her in her home.

In their pursuit to catch the two murderous thugs responsible for both offences Harry and Andrew flew to Larnaca, Cyprus to work in conjunction with the chief of police there, Chief Yiannis Galanis. They had received word the two men plus their boss Mr Nico Castellanos were taking refuge there.

The day they arrived Andrew was violently abducted from his room by the aforementioned two men - the abductors wrongly believing they had taken Harry. You may have heard the BBC News bulletins about two Cypriot men being shot dead, one by a British detective the other by the Chief of Nicosia Police. What they couldn't specify however was it was Andrew who had shot one of the men and Harry himself was shot in the chest, his life being spared only by his bullet proof vest.

He was thrown violently backwards however with the force of the bullet, resulting in him banging his head on a jagged boulder. He subsequently spent several days in hospital recovering from a very serious head wound. That is all I am prepared to say on the matter. Case closed!"

DCS Street took a few sips of water. "Now, as a result of Harry's full, active career and unblemished service, he has requested to take the retirement he is entitled to with effect from today ... Very well done Harry! We will all miss you!"

Genuine heart felt applause filled the office. John Street waited respectfully for it to stop before going on ...

"And now to Andrew, who has only been with us for a short period, primarily to gain experience in detective work.

A famous American once wrote, 'Man is the only animal that blushes - or needs to.'

Well when Andrew first came to us he blushed. My word did he blush! But not anymore. I am sure he gained much experience and confidence working alongside Harry. There is no doubt his combat training and excellent shooting skills recently saved his life. His quick thinking during a crisis also saved Harry's life.

As a result he has now been requested to return to the London Metropolitan as they want him to join the Special Branch at Scotland Yard. A remarkable achievement. Well done Andrew, and keep it up!"

Andrew grinned from ear to ear, oozing confidence as another round of spontaneous applause and excited chatter filled the room.

"Andrew, I have booked you an open train ticket to London Victoria and transferred it to your phone. Have you thought when you might go back to London?"

"Maybe late Sunday afternoon Angela."

"Oh excellent! In that case would you like to join us all for Sunday lunch before you go? I will book the Old Ship for 1pm."

"Thanks Angela I would appreciate that. The last time I went there was with Harry and Liz, a very special Sunday roast it was too - as good as the ones my mum cooks, and that is saying something! There aren't many who can emulate her Yorkshires!"

"Great, I will book a table for six as John Street and his wife Mary would also like to join us."

Harry announced he just had to go and clear his desk, say goodbye to the lads and sort out an evening to have a pint with them. Liz was then going to drive them on to see Max

Grey. Before that both he and Andrew shook hands with John Street and gave Angela a tender hug.

She became quite overwhelmed, telling them to buzz off before she broke down in tears.

"See you Sunday," she managed to blurt out, "1pm and don't forget!"

Very soon Sunday was upon them. Eugene welcomed them to the Old Ship; John Street introduced Andrew to his wife Mary but Harry and Liz were missing ...

"This is definitely not like Harry," declared Angela, "He's always a stickler for punctuality. Where on earth ..."

"Look all of you, out of the window," interrupted Eugene excitedly.

They all huddled at the window where a gleaming red MGB was just pulling up.

"So that's why they went to see Max!" exclaimed Andrew. "I thought it odd he didn't ask me to drive! That's the very same car he drove from the Brunswick car park at the start of the case."

Harry and Liz came in beaming. "Do you all like her?"

"You dark horse!" Grinned Andrew.

"Max gave me a deal I just couldn't refuse, so now this little beauty is mine!"

Harry and Liz joined the others around the table and ordered a bottle of Grand vin de Bordeaux for themselves and John, on the premise of if you're going to celebrate, do it in style! Angela and Mary had a glass of New Zealand Sauvignon Blanc and Andrew an iced Coke. Harry was under strict instructions from Liz to just have the one small glass as he was driving.

Eugene asked if everyone would like the Sunday roast, to a chorus of yes pleases.

Then Andrew suddenly stood up; cleared his throat loudly; leaned across the table; pinched his nostrils together; paused for a second; picked up Harry's glass and downed his wine in one gulp! Screwing his face up like the infamous Gurning Face Guy from Preston as he did so.

Everyone looked on in amazement as he announced ... "Well, in honour of Lewis Carroll, Chief Yiannis Galanis and a friendly bet I made with Harry, it was just calling out - D R I N K   M E ! ! " smiled Andrew.

Harry laughed as he explained to the others, "It's a bet we made on the plane out of Cyprus. Andrew lost the said bet so has just done the honourable thing! Very droll Andrew, well done! It should have been beer but wine is acceptable too."

"Which begs the question Harry, did you ever remember where that saying came from you used at the start of the case, 'If you don't know where you are going any road will take you there'?" asked John Street.

"No Sir, I clean forgot about that!"

"You could hazard a good guess Harry," smiled Andrew. "I'm sure the DCS has always known the answer though!"

"Known what?" puzzled Harry perplexed.

"That Chief Galanis has a penchant if not obsession with literary phrase and quotes!"

"Go on then Andrew, you explain," smiled John Street.

"Well, I think at that point you knew we would be going to Cyprus to follow this case up Sir and you also knew of Chief Galanis's love of Lewis Carroll."

"Brilliant Andrew, yes! From Alice in Wonderland of course. Everyone paraphrases it as Harry did but it is in actual fact a conversation between two characters - Alice and the Cheshire Cat."

Everyone applauded Andrew as Harry poured himself a glass of wine to replace the one Andrew had pinched.

"He's my prodigy!" he then announced proudly.

The meals were devoured with relish as was the cheese and biscuits which followed.

Andrew looked across at Harry who was deep in one of his reveries. "Are you okay?" he asked.

"Yes Andrew I am. I believe I have just resolved our unanswered question ..." Harry called Eugene over and asked if he would mind answering a few questions.

"No of course not Sir."

Harry then asked Andrew to show Eugene the photo of Dimitris Pantazis on his mobile. "Do you know this man?" Harry asked him.

"Yes Sir, he had lunch here a few times. He invariably paid in euros and always gave me a €20 tip."

"Did Winnie ever have her lunch in here at the same time as him?"

"Yes Sir, on the first occasion they simply exchanged pleasantries. The second time he bought her a glass of wine which I took to her table and I'm certain when he came in next he asked her to sit at his table and paid for her lunch."

"Andrew, please show Eugene the photo of Winnie's note book."

"Got it!" Replied Andrew, "I thought you might ask me that!"

"Did you ever see Winnie with this notebook Eugene?"

"Yes Sir, in fact I have one too!" He produced an identical book from his pocket. "Winnie told me she bought it in the newsagent just past The Grand as they were on sale there, so I bought myself one. It's very useful as it fits nicely in my back pocket."

"Did you by any chance see Winnie with it when she had lunch in here with Mr Pantazis?"

"Yes Sir, I saw him write his name and phone number in her book."

"Do you think he knew what Winnie did?"

"Oh yes Sir! When Winnie left the restaurant and thanked him for buying her lunch, we both watched as she made for the ladies toilets then came out in her old clothes. He remarked, 'What a remarkable woman'. I don't think he ever came in here again Sir." Eugene added.

"The last time I saw Winnie was when she had enough money to buy a full meal instead of just the bar snack. Will that be all Sir?"

"Yes, thank you Eugene you have just fitted the very last piece into our puzzle!"

Andrew sat with his mouth wide open. "I'm truly amazed Harry. You never, ever give up do you?" he admired, "so now the case is well and truly closed!" John and Angela gave a little clap.

Harry then felt in his shirt and pulled out a small leather pouch. "I would like you to be custodian of my special keys now Andrew. Guard them with your life as they could get you out of many a fix as they have me.

I always keep them in my shirt pocket so you will have to buy shirts with pockets from now on!"

Andrew was visibly choked at the gesture. He never expected that.

"When. I get settled in the Special Branch Harry and Newcastle are playing Brighton, I will call in to see you all ... mind you," he pondered, "if I'm travelling incognito you won't recognise me will you?"

"Only when you speak with your Newcastle accent Andrew," laughed Harry.

"Och aye," replied Andrew, but I may well change it to Scottish!"

Everyone laughed. "Away with you lad," said John, "go catch your train and I hope all goes well for you. I expect I will receive a review of how well you are progressing through my contact at the Metropolitan HQ."

Andrew said his farewells with hugs for the ladies and a firm handshake from the men.

"We're going for a jaunt to Worthing in the MGB to have a gander at the Bowls Club then on the way back stop at the Meeting Place to watch the Pétanque. I'm still not sure which to take up - I might even join both clubs," Harry pondered.

John, Mary and Angela wished him a happy retirement.

"Well," Liz chipped in, "he will be kept busy there's no doubt about that! You don't want me to get my man in anymore do you dear? ..."

They all chuckled as they went their separate ways.

Chapter 19

D R I N K *to* M E !!

Three months later, when Harry was in the garage polishing the MGB's bonnet, Liz came bursting in waving an envelope. "Look at this Harry, it's a wedding invitation ...

It was on very expensive paper with classy embossed writing:

Mrs Angie Sakalis

Requests the pleasure of Mr & Mrs H Webb

To the wedding of her daughter

Chloe Athena Sakalis to Mr Andrew Gilbert Brown

at the Hotel Eigna, Kato, Paphos, Cyprus

on 2nd May 2023

Please reply asap to:

Mrs Angie Sakalis

Villa Alexelio, Amathus, Limassol, District 4533

"Well, that's a lovely surprise Liz, a really lovely surprise! We will all take the Micky out of him though for his middle name - Gilbert eh! He kept that one quiet!"

"Can we reply 'Yes' and book a two week holiday over there Harry?"

"Of course Liz, why not! There is so much to see and it's such a lovely island. I can introduce you to my friend Zaikai and you can sample for yourself his fantastic food!"

Harry went into raptures, "Oh, his Kleftiko lamb ... well there's nothing quite like it! Nothing at all - well, except for his Stifado beef of course - and you would just love his homemade Moussaka Liz."

At that moment Harry's mobile rang. It was a very excited Angela. "Have you received an invitation to Andrew and Chloe's wedding? It's such wonderful news! I have just taken a call from John Street - they have an invitation too and apparently Yiannis Galanis is giving the bride away!"

"I've just had a thought Angela, do you know the name of Angie Sakalis's second hotel by any chance?"

"Yes, Hotel Eolhc."

"I guessed that's what it would be!"

"No! It's not possible! How could you guess that Harry?"

"It's 'Chloe' spelt backwards, just as Hotel Eigna is 'Angie' spelt backwards!"

"That's so clever and trust you to work it out! I'm going to start saving up and take a week's holiday over there. You never know I might just meet a tall, tanned Cypriot man with a few euros or even diamonds in the bank!"

"Well good luck with that Angela - but if you do just make sure he hasn't a white streak running through his hair!"

They both laughed ...

The End

My sincere thanks to my editor and co-writer Chris Saunders.

Without her help I could not have finished this book. I hope everyone enjoyed reading it.

Malcolm C Brooks

Footnote 1

At the Wedding Ceremony Yiannis Galanis read Shakespeare's
Sonnet 18
For young Chloe certainly was Andrew's
'Darling Bride of May'

Footnote 2

15 months later Chloe would give birth to an 8lb 3oz bouncing
baby boy with longish, (well through Andrew's eyes anyway)
jet black hair
They would Christen him 'Harry'

The picture Andrew carries with him in his wallet

Andrew's Run around the wall

1. Hospital
2. House of Representatives
3. Municipal Gardens
4. Cyprus Museum
5. Municipal Theatre
6. Telecommunications Office
7. Paphos Gate

9. Tourist Information Office
10. Post Office
11. Library
12. Haji Georgakis House
13. Archbishopric
14. Museum of Folk Art
15. National Struggle Museum

17. Famagusta Gate
18. Venetian Walls
19. Open Swimming Pool
20. Presidential Palace
— Green Line